W9-BVD-682

point

# Avalanche

Arthur Roth

SCHOLASTIC INC.
New York Toronto London Auckland Sydney

No part of this publication may be reproduced in whole or in part, or stored in a retrieval system, or transmitted in any form or by any means, electronic, mechanical, photocopying, recording, or otherwise, without written permission of the publisher. For information regarding permission, write to Scholastic Inc., 730 Broadway, New York, NY 10003.

ISBN 0-590-42267-7

Copyright © 1979 by Arthur Roth.
All rights reserved. Published by Scholastic Inc. POINT is a registered trademark of Scholastic Inc.

12 11 10 9 8 7 6 5 4 3 9/8 0 2 3 4/9

Printed in the U.S.A. 01

AVALANCHE

# 1

In one smooth, swift motion, fourteen-year-old Christopher Palmer slid his skis to a stop and unshouldered his rifle. He balanced the bolt action .22 against his side, and shook a pair of binoculars out of the case around his neck. Downhill the blurred outlines of a tan body leaped into focus.

*A coyote!*

The animal, unaware of Chris, was pawing furiously at the snow.

Chris let the binoculars drop back to his chest and glanced up at the snow-covered slope that towered above him. On top of the ridge, snow had arched over to form a cresting peak — a white wave frozen at the height of its curl. Chris knew this part of Idaho well. It was avalanche country. Two years before, a rancher and his horse had been caught in a snowslide. It had been three weeks before their bodies were found.

Still, the snow on the ridge looked fairly compact. And it didn't look deep enough to make much of a slide, even if it did break loose.

Chris put the thought of snowslides out of his mind. He loaded the gun, then slowly raised it to his shoulder. He centered the tip of the front sight in the middle of the back sight V. His finger tightened on the trigger, then relaxed again. He lowered the rifle. He would try to work in a little closer.

It was Easter vacation. Salmon Springs High School was closed, and Chris was spending this Good Friday morning on a cross-country ski jaunt — with a little hunting thrown in.

"Bring back something for the pot," his father had said, and already Chris had three fat grouse jammed in his backpack.

As he shoved off, skiing slowly and

cautiously downhill across the open slope, Chris argued with himself about shooting the coyote. He half hoped the animal would spot him and go bounding off. After all, they had their place as scavengers in the cycle of nature. Still, he had never bagged a coyote, and what mattered to him even more, neither had his hotshot brother, Terry.

Chris slid quietly to a stop and watched the animal for a moment. All that was visible through the plumes of snow being scratched up from the hole was the back half of a gaunt ribbed body. The fur, Chris noticed, was in poor condition. It was a female, probably on her first hunting trip after giving birth to her kits. He felt a quick stab of pity for the mother. Yet he brought the gun to his shoulder. The thrill of the hunt was too strong. He braced himself and, holding his breath, squeezed off a shot.

The animal came alive in a sudden explosion of windmilling limbs. The coyote raced downhill, then hit a pocket of powdery snow and began foundering. She struggled ahead in awkward rising and falling lunges, breasting the snow. Chris gave a whoop of joy. He had her now! He could easily overtake the struggling animal and finish her off.

He had just slewed around on his skis, getting ready to push off, when he felt a strange vibration. At the same moment his ears caught a heavy whooshing sound, like the vague rumble of a far-away thunderstorm. He turned his head to look uphill and the bottom dropped right out of his stomach.

The whole top of the mountain seemed to be crashing down on him. A tumbling wall of snow, filling the air with a fine powdery mist, was building as it roared down. The shot had set off an avalanche. And he was right in its path!

Automatically, he pulled on his leather mittens and pushed off, leaving the gun behind. He reached up and pulled the hood of his jacket over his head, instinctively trying to protect himself from the onrushing horror. Maybe, just maybe, he could out-ski the avalanche. He flew straight downhill. It was at least a thousand feet to the valley floor but maybe he could make it. He might break a leg or an arm trying to stop his cross-country skis at the bottom, but that would be better than being buried alive.

As he sped downhill, Chris tried to remember everything he had heard or read about avalanches. *When the slide hit you,* he recalled, *you were supposed to swim. That would keep you close to the top layer of snow.*

He was halfway down the slope, and thinking that he just might make it, when he felt the ground rise under his feet. At the same time, an arching wave of snow came pounding down over his head. He had a glimpse of towering plumes of snow, then darkness descended. The heavy binoculars flew up and banged him on the nose. He grabbed the leather strap and pulled the glasses up over his head. With his arms now raised, he began to swim in the all-enveloping whiteness. He kept his teeth locked and tried to breathe through his nose. He knew that he would suffocate if he got too much fine snow into his lungs. For several awful moments he was on his back, his skis above him. At times he lost all sense of where his body was in relation to the ground.

A sudden searing pain knifed through his chest and he realized that he had sucked a mouthful of snow into his lungs. He bit down hard. His legs, caught in their skis, dragged him down. Still he kept urging himself to swim, kept windmilling his arms. He imagined he was climbing a flight of stairs and used his whole body to try and fight his way upward out of the smothering world of fine powdery snow.

Finally he felt his forward motion slow down. The whole burden of snow was coming to rest. Chris felt himself sink deeper and deeper. After a final settling movement of snow somewhere above him, all was still and quiet.

The sudden eerie stillness was even more terrifying than the roar of the snow in motion. Cautiously Chris opened his eyes. He drew in several shallow breaths through his nose, then terror took over. He began to scream. But in his desperate struggle to free himself he became aware that there was some air. There had to be, he was breathing. And as far as he could tell, he was standing upright. He soon realized that struggling would use up whatever air was available, and it might cause his body to settle deeper into the snow.

He forced himself to be calm. He thought

of his mother and father and his brother, Terry. What were they doing right now? What would they say when they heard the news of his death?

"I'm going to die," Chris said aloud in his snow tomb. His panic rose again as he listened to himself pass this sentence of death on Christopher Palmer. You smothered to death in an avalanche, he told himself. There wasn't enough air to breathe under six, or sixteen, or sixty feet of snow. Or did you freeze to death? Either way, it didn't matter—you just didn't come out alive.

But he wasn't smothering, not yet anyway. He moved his head from left to right, then up and down, trying to clear a pocket of space in front of his face. He managed, by pressing up against the snow, to slide the hood of his jacket back off his head.

He was suddenly very tired. He closed his eyes and let his head drop down on his chest. He would grab a short nap, then he would figure some way out of this jam. He was okay . . . all he needed was a quick rest . . . a short sleep . . . then he'd be ready to face anything. He'd find some way out . . . don't worry.

As the air in the small clear space around his head grew foul, Chris began to have hallucinations. He dreamed it was the middle of summer and he was eight years old again. It was that first summer after he recovered from scarlet fever, and everyone was spoiling him. He and Mom and Dad were on a picnic at Lodgepole Lake. Terry wasn't with them. Chris was wandering in the woods, following a huge red coyote. The red coyote would trot ahead a few steps, then stop to look back. Chris had to hurry to keep up.

The coyote sat down and waited. Chris tried to hurry. Then the animal opened its mouth. The jaws opened wider, the red, raw mouth got larger and larger, until everything else was blotted out. There were no trees, no mountains, no sky — only the huge jaws that completely enclosed him.

That was the last thing Chris Palmer remembered before he blacked out.

# 2

That morning, Chris had come down to breakfast earlier than usual. His mother had turned around from the stove when she heard him come into the kitchen. "It's easy to see there's no school today," she greeted him. "Otherwise I would have had to drag you out of bed."

Chris grinned at her. Then he raised his voice to be heard above the noise coming from the laundry room. "Good morning, Dad!"

His father grunted something, then came stamping into the kitchen rubbing his hands together. "The only trouble with

Easter coming early is that it still seems wintertime," he said, sitting down. "Radio says chance of scattered snow showers this afternoon and early evening."

Chris's father worked for the highway department as assistant superintendent of highways for the town of Salmon Springs. He worried a lot about the weather, especially winter storms that blocked his highways.

"Did you take up the snow fences yet?" Chris asked.

"No, it's too early."

"Then relax. It won't snow as long as the snow fences are still up."

Jack Palmer laughed. He reached for a piece of toast and spread it thick with honey.

"Terry up yet?" he asked, between mouthfuls.

"No," Molly Palmer answered. "Let him sleep for a while. He's still a growing boy."

"Eats like one, that's for sure. You know that boy outweighs me?"

"Big deal," Chris said. "So he's fat."

Chris's father came to the defense of his older son. "What do you mean, fat? That's all muscle. Listen, the guy is built like a Big Ten linebacker."

"Not like me, huh, Dad?" There was a hint of bitterness in the voice. Chris was tall and thin, lank and loose, all skin and bones.

Jack Palmer put up his hands. "Now I didn't say that. You got the brains in the family — Terry's got the brawn."

"I think you have an interesting build," his mother said. She was setting out milk, sugar, cornflakes, spoons, and bowls.

Father and son looked at each other and burst out laughing.

"Interesting?" Jack Palmer asked. "What kind of a build is an *interesting* build?"

"Ma, you're too much," Chris said.

"What I mean is, more interesting for girls," Molly Palmer explained. "Girls aren't *always* attracted to men with muscles." She sat down and shook some cornflakes into a blue enameled bowl. "Take your father there," she said. "Why, he was positively scrawny when I first met him."

"I was *not* scrawny," Jack Palmer objected. "I was slim and supple and . . ."

"Lithe," Chris supplied.

"Lithe, that's it. I was a lean and mean machine. Don't forget, I was on the wrestling team in college."

"When I first met your father," Molly Palmer said, "he was positively scrawny. He used to bring his lunch to work every day and his lunch was always the same: one bologna sandwich, one apple, and one chocolate cupcake in a brown paper bag. Do you know what first attracted me to your father?" she asked.

"No, Ma, what?"

"Curiosity," she replied. "You see, when he was finished with his lunch, he used to fold up the paper bag and put it in his jacket pocket. He used the same bag for weeks."

"Sounds just like you, Dad," Chris said. "You still save empty bags."

"I don't see the point in throwing useful things away," Jack Palmer answered.

"That's why we have a barn full of useful things," his wife joked. She sprinkled sugar on her cornflakes and continued: "I knew it was the same brown paper bag because it had an oily stain on one side the shape of Texas. He used to fold the bag every day, nice and neat, so that Texas was always on the outside. After two weeks of that, I simply had to find out what made him so neat and methodical."

"Your mother was actually my boss," Jack Palmer said. "I used to work for her in the public library. I'd report to her first thing in the morning and she'd tell me what to do. What do you think of that, son?"

"Fantastic, Dad."

"I was curious about such a methodical man," Mrs. Palmer repeated.

"So what did you do, Ma?" Chris usually asked this question at this point in the story.

"The next payday I invited him out to lunch," Molly Palmer said.

"So I had a salami on rye instead of a bologna on white," her husband teased. "And the next night was a Saturday and I took her to a fire department dance and we both lived happily ever after."

They smiled at each other, and Chris quickly changed the subject. "Don't you get Good Friday off, Dad?"

"Half a day, from noon. What are your plans for the Easter vacation?"

"I thought I'd get in a last bit of skiing before the weather warms up too much. I'll take the twenty-two and go along by Frenchman's Flats. See if I can pick up a few grouse."

"You don't have a rehearsal today?" his mother asked.

Chris shook his head. "Not until Monday night. Then it's every night next week and the week after."

Chris had a small part in the high school play. They were doing *Hamlet* and had been rehearsing for over a month. He had never been in a more difficult play. In fact, all the kids were complaining that it was too hard. But Mr. Spiker, the new English teacher, had insisted on doing Shakespeare and he had finally talked the kids into *Hamlet.*

"How's the play coming?" Mrs. Palmer asked.

"It's a disaster," Chris said. "Half the time I don't even know what the words mean."

"Didn't the teacher explain the play to you?" his father asked.

"Oh sure, but it's not the same thing. Some of the lines are really hard to say." Chris threw out his hands and recited: "Ah, excellent good friends! How dost thou, Guildenstern? Ah, Rosencrantz! Good lads, how do you both?"

His parents laughed at his exaggerated reading of the lines.

"They sure talked weird back in those days," Chris complained.

"I'm sure they'd think we talk weird, if they could hear us," his mother pointed out.

"I suppose," Chris admitted.

"Don't forget, you promised your mother that you and Terry would paint your room over Easter vacation."

"We'll do it on Monday, Dad. That's if Idaho's Great Olympic Hope doesn't have track or baseball practice."

"I'll see that he helps you," Jack Palmer promised.

"Thanks, Dad. You know I can't tell him anything."

"Funny, that's what he says about you." Mr. Palmer glanced up at the kitchen clock. "I'd better leave," he said, draining the last of his coffee. He looked over at his son. "Be careful on those skis and don't stay out too long. There may be a snowstorm on the way."

"I'll watch it, Dad. Don't worry."

"And just remember that your heart's not as strong as you think it is," his mother said.

"Ah, Mom, cut it out," Chris pleaded.

"Doctor Sigler said there was no sign of that heart murmur anymore."

"Yes, and Doctor Rickett said it had gone away when *he* examined you. But three years later it was back."

"For heaven's sake, Molly, stop treating him like a baby."

Mrs. Palmer stood up and angrily pushed back from the table. "Jack, don't give me advice about the children's health."

Jack Palmer's face tightened and Chris could see the anger in his father's eyes.

"Ah, for Pete's sake," Chris said. "I'll look after myself, don't worry. And, Ma, quit dragging up those old stories."

Molly Palmer began clearing off the table. "I don't care what the doctors say. They don't always know best. You simply have to accept the fact that you can't do quite as much as other boys. Maybe in a few years you'll be strong enough to forget about your heart, but for the present just don't overdo."

"Okay, Ma. Okay."

"We have one athlete in the family, that's enough," she declared.

Jack Palmer walked over and kissed his wife on the cheek. "I'd better hurry or I'll be late."

Chris watched his father shrug into his jacket and put on his black wool cap. Watch him now, Chris thought. He won't say good-bye to me. Chris waited until his father had grasped the doorknob, then called after him, "So long, Dad."

"Bye, Ter — I mean Chris." His father turned around and smiled. "Bring back something for the pot."

Chris winced. There it was again — Terry — Hotshot Terry, the star athlete — Terry, the eight-yards-a-carry back, the .400 batting average, the four-thirty-seven mile — Terry of the superlative statistics. It made no difference that he, Chris, was on the Honor Roll, that he was already an editor on the school paper, that in his first year in high school he was making better than a 95 average. With his father, if you didn't do something with a football, or a baseball, or a basketball, then you were a nobody.

"Do you want to take some sandwiches and a thermos of coffee?" his mother asked.

"No, I won't be away that long."

Chris went out to the laundry room and got into his waterproof ski jacket and pants. Then he put on his ski boots. He slipped a small box of .22 shells into one pocket and took the binoculars down from their peg on the wall. He shouldered his way into a knapsack, and finally lifted down the .22.

"Do you want to wait for a while?" his mother asked. "Terry might feel like going with you."

"Naw, let Superman get his sleep. See you later, Mom."

Chris opened the back door of the kitchen and headed for the barn to get his skis. When he came out of the barn, his father was already in the pickup, waiting at the end of the driveway to make the turn onto the county road. The way his father's shoulders were leaning to one side, and the way his head was bent, told Chris that he was trying to tune the radio. He was hoping to pick up another weather report, Chris guessed, and he felt a sudden rush of love for his father.

"Turn around, Dad," he whispered, "and I'll wave to you."

Jack Palmer straightened up, and pulled out smartly onto the highway. At the last moment he spotted his son in the rearview mirror, waving good-bye. He was about to honk the horn in reply, but held off when he noticed an approaching truck. He didn't want the driver of the truck to think that he was blowing the horn at him.

Chris looked away from the road and over to his house. Terry was standing at the window of their bedroom, yawning. Chris realized that Terry must have been watching him wave good-bye to their father. Just as Chris started to wave to his brother, Terry turned away from the window.

Chris shrugged, then pushed forward on his skis, headed for Frenchman's Flats.

# 3

Ski poles digging in on each side of his body, Chris tracked smoothly along the old logging road. He took his time and enjoyed the scenery. He was in no hurry.

It was a good five miles to Frenchman's Flats, an open grassy bowl in the forest, where a French settler back in the last century had tried to carve out a small farm. The settler had hoped to live off the land while he prospected for gold in the surrounding mountains. But during World War I, the Frenchman had abandoned the farm and gone back to his native country to fight.

The grassy bowl, rimmed with evergreens, attracted a lot of grouse. Chris or Terry had yet to ski there and not find some of the birds working the ground for pine needles, or nesting in clumps of sage grass. They ran in family flocks of four to fourteen, fanning out as they scratched at the dirt and grass for insects and juniper berries. Once Chris had picked off six of the plump, brown-speckled birds before the remaining handful took fright and flew off.

Kicking and gliding, swinging his weight onto the leading ski, Chris sped quietly over the smooth snow. From time to time he glanced up at the sky, where a solid bank of gray clouds seemed to be settling lower and lower. So far, though, no snow had fallen. Chris moved in a rhythmic pattern, his skiing almost automatic. The world around was white and silent except for the crisp running hiss from his skis.

He stepped around a fallen tree and slowed his pace a little. In another few hundred yards he would break out of the woods onto Frenchman's Flats. He did not want to alarm any grouse or rabbits. One good thing about hunting on skis, they were practically silent.

He came to a ragged fringe of trees and halted to examine the bare expanse of snow ahead. A few yards in front of him a line of deer tracks crossed the clearing.

Letting the ski poles dangle from their wrist straps, he took the binoculars out and examined the clearing. The snow was at least three days old and criss-crossed with animal tracks. Besides the deer prints, there were the dragging comet-tail tracks of rabbits, the small fan-shaped pads of a coyote or fox, and the stick-figure marks of crows and magpies.

A tiny explosion of brown caught the corner of his eye, and he swung the glasses around to search the brush. Half a dozen grouse were working under a clump of trees, turning over the snow-covered leaves to look for insects.

He moved a few yards closer, then swung the rifle off his shoulder. He swiftly loaded the gun and, resting the barrel against the trunk of a lodgepole pine, he zeroed in on one of the birds. Holding his breath, the stock of the rifle nestled against his cheek, he slowly squeezed the trigger.

*Crack!*

The bird somersaulted once in the air,

then fell back on the snow. One final wing-beat and all movement ceased.

"One," Chris whispered. He moved the rifle barrel to sight in on a second bird.

*Crack!*

This time the birds exploded into flight. Chris thought he had missed, but in mid-flight one bird gave a surprised "*crawwwwk!*" and tumbled out of the air as the others fled in long sloping glides. Chris's eyes searched the lower limbs of the pines and hemlock that ringed the clearing for more birds. Finally he spotted one, perched on the branch of a ragged hemlock tree.

*Crack!*

The bird silently dropped from its perch. Chris decided that three grouse were enough. He unloaded the gun, skied forward to collect his birds, then wrung their necks to make sure they were dead. Then he packed them away in his knapsack. He was barely able to get the flap closed. They would make a nice dinner for the whole family, especially the way Mom cooked them — in a wine stew with lots of carrots and potatoes and onions. Just thinking about it made him hungry.

He crossed the clearing, taking pleasure in the way his skis drew parallel lines through the open field of snow. From time to time he glanced up at the heavy threatening sky. The snow had held off. He ought to turn around and go home. He had probably done enough for the day.

Still he wasn't tired, and he was enjoying himself. He decided to stay out for another hour at least. It might be the last chance he would have to ski cross-country until next winter.

Chris thought then of Hidden Lake, higher up in the mountains. It was isolated because of the dense brush and briar that covered the nearby slopes. This was another great thing about skis, he decided. Sometimes you could ski right over thorns and brush that you would have to battle through in the summer.

The thing that excited Chris about Hidden Lake was that no one had ever seen it frozen over. The people around Salmon Springs had a theory that warm springs fed directly into the lake, keeping the water from freezing. The occasional forest ranger or hunter who visited the lake never bothered to go there in winter. But they had been there in spring and late fall, and had never found any ice on the lake, even though the temperature was cold enough.

It would take, Chris guessed, about two hours of steady skiing to reach the lake. He could come back in half the time because the return trip would be mostly downhill. Imagine the surprise of everyone — his dad, Hotshot Terry — when he hit them with the news that he had skied into Hidden Lake!

Chris swung steadily along, jabbing with his poles. Maybe Ma wouldn't like it, but Terry and Dad would sure be surprised. Maybe, too, Dad would begin to realize that Chris was every bit as good as Terry in *some* things. Let's face it, he was a better cross-country skier than Terry, and a trip into Hidden Lake would prove it.

But supposing it began to snow? Well, if it did, Chris decided, he would turn back. If he backtracked at the first sign of snow, he would have plenty of time to reach home safely.

His mind made up, he pushed ahead and an hour later came to a long open slope on the side of a mountain. He halted for a moment to look up at the top of the ridgeline, where a high over-burden of snow was frozen into the shape of a wave.

A flicker of motion caught his eye, drawing his attention away from the ridge. He swung his head and looked down the slope that fell away below him.

Was that an animal of some sort?

He reached for his binoculars. . . .

# 4

"I'm drowning! I'm drowning!" Chris was struggling back to consciousness. No matter how hard he worked his lungs, he couldn't seem to get enough air. He sucked in desperately, then threw back his head and screamed. "Help me, somebody! Help me!" He tried frantically to claw himself free from the snow.

The panic passed as soon as he realized his screams were doing no good. Forcing himself to calm down, he took stock of his situation. His arms and legs were held tight, but he could rock his head back and forth.

He set to work to clear more space around his face. Soon he was able to push back and look upward through the dim gray light that filtered down. High above, perhaps six feet over his head, he could see a small round hole through which poured a ray of bright sunshine. Above the hole a patch of blue was visible.

"The sky!" he cried out. "I can see the sky!"

The sight lifted his spirits. He felt a flood of gratitude. He had a pipeline to the surface air. The sun must have melted through a thin spot in the snow cover. And just in time too; he could not have lasted much longer in the oxygen-poor air of his prison.

But how long could he survive? He realized he had to have three things: food, water, and air. For the moment he had air. For water he could bite out a few mouthfuls of snow and melt them. He hadn't brought any food, but with plenty of air and water he could last a few days at least. The big problem was that no one knew where he was. His family wouldn't start looking for him until late afternoon at the earliest. Perhaps they might even wait until the following morning before they began their search. They knew he had gone to Frenchman's Flats. From there they would pick up his ski tracks leading to Hidden Lake.

Even if they waited until morning, they should reach the avalanche site by tomorrow afternoon at the latest. As soon as they reached the snowslide, they would know what had happened. They would work through the piled-up masses of snow with their poles, probing for his body. All he had to do was hang on for twenty-four hours. The thought sent another wave of panic over him, and he began to shudder. Then he went rigid, biting his lip until he finally got control of his fear. If he was going to last twenty-four hours in this snow cell, he would have to control his hysteria.

If he had only taken the sandwiches and coffee Mom had offered him. If he had only turned back when he reached Frenchman's Flats. If he had only not seen that coyote. Or not shot at it. If he had only not gone skiing this morning. If only . . . if only . . .

Chris felt another shudder run through his body. His nerves were strung taut. Curious, he thought, that so far he had not really felt the cold. Of course he was well sheltered from any wind, and he supposed the snow also acted as a sort of insulation. His body heat probably warmed up the air around him, at least enough to keep him from freezing. Except perhaps for his feet. He just hoped that they wouldn't get frost-bitten.

He tried to bend from the waist, to lever the upper half of his body forward a couple of inches. It was difficult to move — still he could be worse. Suppose he had ended up stretched out on his back! Or had come to rest upside down! He couldn't have lasted even an hour then. At least being upright gave him some sort of a chance.

He bent again at the waist and tried to rock back and forth. After half an hour's hard rocking around the upper half of his body, he managed to compress enough snow to add another couple of inches clearance.

Suddenly anxious about the air hole, he tilted back his head to look up. The sunlight was more slanting now. The sun had passed its meridian. It was already afternoon. He wondered what time it was. He had a digital watch, but unless he could free his arms there was no way he could see it.

There was a possibility that he could work his arms loose, but there was still no way he could free his legs with the skis so firmly bound to his feet. It was hopeless. The best thing was not to struggle, to save his strength and hope that he could last until someone reached him tomorrow.

Perhaps he should try to sleep for a while. He might have to do a lot of shouting tomorrow, and he ought to save his strength until he was sure that people were nearby and searching for him.

He closed his eyes and his thoughts turned to his family. What would they think when he didn't come home? Suppose he died. How would Mom and Dad take it? And Terry, how would he react? Old Terry would miss him, but wouldn't he also be a bit relieved? There wouldn't be anyone else whose grades they would hold up to him for comparison. And Terry would have the whole bedroom to himself. He could fill the walls on Chris's side of the room with all kinds of sports charts.

Chris tried to will himself to sleep. Instead of counting sheep, he went over some of the lines in the play. He thought of Hamlet's death speech. How did it go?

Slowly he began to recite: *"Oh I die, Horatio,* something, something. *I cannot live to hear the news of England . . ."*

The words moved him as they had never moved him before in any of the rehearsals. Then he remembered Horatio's final words: *"Now cracks a noble heart. Good night sweet Prince and flights of angels sing thee to thy rest."*

Chris's eyes filled with tears, and he began furiously to rock his body back and forth, trying to struggle out of his snow tomb.

"Get me out of here!" he yelled, over and over again.

# 5

"They'll find me, first thing in the morning they're sure to find me," Chris said aloud. It was full night now — blackness, like blindness, everywhere. The night hours would be the worst, he knew. He was sure that the snow was going to collapse down around his head and smother him.

"They'll find me. They'll find me, all right," he said again and again into the darkness. "Eeeny meeny miney mo!" he sang aloud. "They will find me in the snow!" To block out thoughts of smothering and to keep his mind busy, he began to do mathematical problems in his head.

After that he recited all the Spanish words he knew. Then he sang all the songs he knew. He was even able to grin at the thought of a passerby walking over the air hole and hearing singing deep within the snow.

Through the worst parts of the night, Chris held on to one thought: His folks were organizing a rescue team. By first light in the morning at least a dozen people would be out searching for him. All he had to do was hang on for another few hours. By noon, at the latest, someone would reach him.

Toward morning the air in his snow prison turned bad again. For periods of five minutes or more, Chris found himself panting strenuously. Despite all the snow around him, he felt hot and wondered if he was running a fever. That was all he needed, he groaned, to come down with pneumonia or some illness like that.

Gradually the blackness around him turned gray and he was able to make out the walls of his prison. The first thing that struck him was that he had more space immediately above his head. His body had settled a good six inches during the night, faster than the surrounding snow was settling. There was also more clear space around his arms and shoulders. The settling snow had drawn away from him somewhat.

He looked up, but he couldn't see his air hole. Perhaps it was still too early. Was the sun not up yet? He had no way of knowing the time. He had still not been able to free his arms to look at his wristwatch.

He started moving his left shoulder up and down, trying to clear more space. Then he doubled up his left hand, made a fist, and punched downward. Half a dozen punches and he could feel a definite cracking of the icy shield that had formed around his body during the night.

He took a rest then and thought about what he was doing. He was going about things the wrong way, he decided. He ought to free his best arm — his right arm — first. Then he could use that arm to reach across to his left hip, and get his hunting knife. With the hunting knife out, he could carve more space for himself. He could even free his left arm and finally get to his watch.

Rejuvenated by this plan of action, he

began moving his right arm up and down, fanning his elbow in and out, like a wing, and moving his shoulder back and forth. It took a lot of work, but a last desperate wriggle of the right side of his body loosened his arm. Suddenly his right hand was up and in front of his face.

He was so excited, he almost cried. It was as though a familiar friend had come to pay him a visit and share his problems. He pulled the leather mitten off with his teeth, then repeated the operation with the inner wool glove. The glove and mitten he stuck inside the neck of his jacket.

His hand might be numb and half frozen, but it looked beautiful. He stared at the long, slender fingers, the nails smoothly rounded, the thumb perfectly shaped. He waggled the fingers a bit and spoke to the hand. "Hello, hand!" The hand nodded back to him, patted his cheeks, his nose, his lips. Then he squirmed the hand down inside his wool shirt and undershirt and let it nest in the hollow of his left armpit.

While he was warming his hand, he leaned back and looked up. He still couldn't locate the opening. Puzzled, he stared up at the cone of snow for a moment before the fact fully struck home. The air hole was blocked! It must have snowed again during the night!

Chris dropped his head and groaned with despair. He should have realized. It had been getting harder to breathe, but he assumed it was because of all his physical activity. Now it was evident that not enough air was filtering down to him.

Before he could do anything about it, though, he had to relieve himself. He was really in pain. He pushed his hand down through the snow, found the tab of his zipper, and unzipped his pants. He wrinkled his nose at the harsh smell that rose from his urine. That didn't help to make the air any purer. One thing it did do, though — it melted away some of the snow around his legs.

When he was through, he zipped up his pants and put the glove and mitten back on. He used his teeth as a vise as he worked each finger into its individual compartment. Then he snaked his hand up in front of his face, stretching the arm and hand and fingers as high as they would go. In this way he managed to make a narrow tunnel up through the snow.

Unfortunately, he was still short of the surface, a good three or four feet, he guessed. If he could only get to his knife, he could extend his upward reach another six inches or so. But that would still leave him a couple of feet short of breaking through. If he had only held on to one of his ski poles. Or if only he had a breathing tube that he could poke up through the snow and into the air above. He had read that Indians used to hide from their enemies in creeks and rivers that way. They would sink themselves under the water and use a hollow reed, sticking above the surface, to breathe through.

As the air got worse, he grew sleepy. But he was afraid to close his eyes for fear he would go into a coma. Above all, he wanted to stay awake until noon. By then he expected someone to find him.

He began to drift off. It was so hard to keep his eyes open. Maybe he should try to free his left arm and get to his watch. He thrust his hand inside his jacket and let his head drop to his chest. He would just close his eyes for a second or so. A five-minute nap surely wouldn't do any harm. . . .

When he woke up, he was patting the snow in front of his face. For a moment he was disoriented. Then with a terrible sense of despair, he realized where he was. He was like a condemned man in jail who dreams of an earlier, happier time when he was free, then wakes up to the knowledge that he has only a few days to live.

Chris wasn't with his family — that was a dream. He was all by himself in the mountains, trapped under tons of snow, with perhaps only hours to live if help didn't reach him soon.

He leaned back and looked up. His bitter disappointment on waking up was lessened by the sight of a tiny ray of sunshine. His surface pocket was open again, and the air smelled cool and fresh. The fresh air was probably what woke him. Now if he could just find a way to keep this lifeline open through the snow-banked roof.

He forced his right hand downward and across the front of his waist. He would get to his hunting knife and try to free his other arm. It was only then that he realized the full significance of that fall of snow during the night. His ski tracks were now covered with fresh snow. His rescuers had no way of tracking him!

"Oh no!" he moaned. "No! No! No! That's not fair!"

# 6

"Are you anything to Terry Palmer?" the man asked.

"He's my brother," Chris replied.

"He's some athlete, that kid," the man said.

"Yeah, I guess," Chris agreed.

Chris didn't know how many times he had had that conversation with people. Sometimes he was even introduced as "Terry Palmer's kid brother." It was really a pain coming three years behind a brother who was a famous high school sports star. It was especially bad for Chris because people expected him to be good in sports, and he wasn't. He wasn't even average.

Of course that heart murmur had held him back. But even if he were a hundred percent fit, he didn't think he could compete with Terry. He didn't mind all that much, except that sometimes he suspected that Terry was contemptuous of him. His brother never said anything, but Chris often felt that Terry was ashamed of him. This made Chris study that much harder, and it sometimes made him sarcastic about his brother's intelligence. Terry was just an average student.

Chris opened his eyes and looked around his gray prison. Snow, cold, avalanche. Somehow he had slept again. He didn't know how long, but it felt like hours. It was the first real sleep he had managed since the snowslide had swept him away. He glanced up at the air hole and guessed, from the amount of light filtering down, that it was late afternoon.

His father and brother would have been out since early morning looking for him. But now that the overnight fall of snow had wiped out his tracks, they would have no way of knowing that Chris had gone on to Hidden Lake. They would probably search all the valleys and draws to the east of Frenchman's Flats first. Then they would assume that he had moved on down to the lower foothills.

Chris wondered if he should try shouting. But he doubted he could be heard more than a few feet away. Someone would have to be standing right over the air hole. He might as well save his breath. What he ought to do next, he decided, was free his left hand so that he could make use of his knife and get to his watch.

He was very thirsty. He scooped out a few handfuls of snow from the bank in front of him and let the snow melt in his mouth until his thirst faded. After that he went to work on freeing his left arm.

An hour or so later he had both arms free and was thawing out his left hand inside his shirt. When his hand was warm, he pressed the time button on the digital watch on his left wrist. Fortunately the watch was working and flashed 6:11 in tiny red numerals.

It had taken quite a while to thaw out his left hand, which made him really worried about his feet. At first they had felt terribly cold, then gradually feeling had left his toes until there was no longer any sensation in his feet at all. His toes might be frostbitten already. He tried to move his legs, but found it almost impossible. Then he tried to arch his feet inside the ski boots and flex his toes. There was some response but he was afraid that after another night trapped in the snow his feet would be completely frozen. As it was, they felt like chunks of stone.

He was the wrong Palmer for this situation. By now Terry would have set up an elaborate series of exercises to keep all parts of his body functioning. Chris smiled as he thought of the charts tacked to the walls on Terry's side of their bedroom: running charts — how many laps he ran each day, his greatest number per day, per week, per month; his best time for the 100, 220, 440, the half, and the mile; his seasonal batting average, his slugging percentages, his fielding averages; his yards per carry and his field goal percentages. Chris often marveled at his brother's bookkeeping. He kidded Terry about it, saying that his brother was sure to be an accountant one day. And although Terry claimed to be terrible in math, he could still, in a flash, work out his batting average to three decimal points.

Suddenly Chris felt an overwhelming rush of love for his brother, that brother with whom he had so often fought, his rival for their father's affection. If it was difficult to have a brother who was a natural athlete, then surely it was just as difficult to have a brother who was a whiz at math and English and languages. It couldn't have been easy for Terry, either.

Chris felt tears in his eyes. School was tough on Terry. He had to work hard just to get average grades. If he came out of this alive, Chris promised himself, one of the first things he would do would be to tell his brother how much he admired him. *And I do*, Chris thought, *I really do.*

To prove his admiration, his love, Chris decided to do what Terry would have done in the same situation. He would set up a schedule of exercises to keep his body in as good shape as possible. He would start by arching his feet, then flexing his toes, then trying to exercise the muscles in his calves and thighs. He would do this twenty-five times every hour.

He checked his watch again. Five minutes to seven. He began to arch his feet, then tried to flex and spread his toes. He found it difficult at first, and he had to will himself to move his foot muscles. After a while, though, the exercise developed a natural rhythm and by the time he reached twenty-five, he had decided to try a new exercise — running in place. He began by flexing his knees, swinging his hips, moving his shoulders, springing up off his ankles, everything a runner does except actually lifting his feet off the ground. After a while his legs and feet were all pins and needles. The feeling was one of painful pleasure, pleasure that his feet could experience feeling again, and pain as the blood began dilating the veins.

He ran in place until he felt sweat bead his forehead. The exercises sent a warm glow throughout his body. He hoped that running would keep his legs and feet from getting frostbitten, and that was important. Who wanted to survive if it meant losing your legs, or even your feet? But he was worried, too, that the exercises would use up his energy reserves too fast. He was taking in no calories. How long could he last without food?

But he *had* food! Of course! He had those three grouse in his knapsack. He could eat them, if he could just get to them. The knapsack was resting on the small of his back. He would have a rough time getting it pulled around. And he wondered if he could unhook the flap, even if he got the knapsack right in front of him. The sack had been bulging. He remembered that he had just barely managed to work the prong of the buckle through the last hole in the strap.

The exercises had tired him out. He would give up on the grouse for now. Time to rest again, if he could. At least now he realized he had a source of food. And somehow he would get that knapsack open.

He drifted off to sleep, dreaming of three grouse sizzling on a spit over a charcoal fire.

# 7

"Wait for me. Hey, wait!" Chris cried out. But his brother picked up the pace and drew steadily away from him.

"You're a cripple!" Terry called back to him. "You can't run. You've got a bad heart!"

Chris was furious. His legs churned at the grass of the quarter mile track behind the high school. He would show Terry. He would . . .

He woke up with his legs feebly jerking. He had no idea how long he had slept. He dragged his left arm up to look at his watch. He pressed the time button: 9:20.

Then he pressed the button again to get the date. Nothing flashed on the tiny black screen. He pressed the time button once again: 9:21. Then once again he pressed the button. Still no response. The damp must have knocked out part of the system. The watch was giving him hours and minutes, and even seconds, but not the date and month.

He felt confused. Was it the first or second day of his imprisonment? He was starting his second night, wasn't he? He would have to make some kind of calender, some sort of mark in the snow. He didn't want to lose track of the days. The avalanche was Friday. This was Saturday.

Tomorrow then was Sunday, Easter Sunday. He was lucky it was the Easter weekend. More people would have time off and be free to look for him. Practically the whole highway department would be out helping his dad. Who else? Most of his high school class would volunteer. The police of course — not only the Salmon Springs Police, but also the County and State Police — and the fire department and the rangers in the Forest Service. There would be plenty of volunteers out beating the bushes for him. That is, if the weather stayed fair. He just hoped that a heavy snowstorm didn't hit the area. If it snowed again, it would mean the end for him.

He decided to do his running exercises again, but he soon got dizzy, and had to stop. He began again, and again he got dizzy. Then he accidentally found a cure. He was all right if he kept his eyes closed. He finally ran five hundred paces, which he guessed was a quarter mile. When the running was over, and his legs and feet were tingling, he put them to work in a mental game of one-on-one basketball with Terry. Because it was a make-believe game, he allowed himself to score the winning basket with a falling away, one-handed hookshot from just beyond the circle.

Of course Terry would laugh at the idea of Chris beating him in a game of one-on-one basketball. And so would his dad. But then Dad had always favored Terry over Chris, just as Mom loved him more than Terry. The problem was that Chris would rather be his father's favorite. He didn't like his mother always babying him. But then Terry hadn't caught scarlet fever when he was a kid.

Chris thought how funny it would be if Terry would rather be his mother's favorite. Maybe he and Terry could swap when he got out of this mess. Did Mom like him more than Terry because she was smarter than Dad? Or was that why Dad liked Terry more? Boy, people were really complicated when you thought about it, especially parents. If he ever got to be a parent, he would make sure that he didn't favor one of his kids over another. He would love them all equally. But maybe that was impossible.

Chris shivered, then lifted his arm up in front of his face. He pressed the time button once again: 11:20. He was so grateful to have his watch. It was like a cellmate, sharing his imprisonment. He should try and get as much sleep as possible during the night. During the day he needed to be alert for the sound of rescuers. First thing in the morning he would have to figure out some way to get at those grouse. That would be his Easter present to himself. Some Easter dinner all right, a raw grouse!

Just when he was settling down to sleep again, after another short round of jogging in place, he was hit with an excruciating pain in the pit of his stomach. Cramp after searing cramp clawed through his intestines. He had never felt such tearing pains before! He grabbed his stomach with both hands to hold in the agony. The wall of his stomach felt as hard as a rock. Sweat formed on his forehead and he pushed his face into the snow and began to moan. Had his appendix burst, or what?

After what seemed like hours of unbearable pain, his bowels loosened and before he could stop himself he had fouled his clothes. The stench was overpowering. He gagged on the smell and almost threw up.

He was in for a long grim night, he realized. And if he kept having attacks like this, he would rather pass out and have done with it. He had never known such stomach pain before. Could all that snow he had eaten be responsible? Maybe he should cut down on the amount of snow he was eating. What else could it have been? Those dizzy spells earlier were probably a warning. Maybe the cramps were a severe form of hunger pain. After all, he had had nothing to eat since breakfast the day before.

"Oh, Mama," he called weakly. "Oh Mama, Mama, I feel so awful."

But no mother came with hot soup. No father came with a gruff joke, and no brother was there to help him through the endless night.

# 8

"Hello up there! Hello out there!" Chris shouted. "Hello, Salmon Springs! Hello, world! Anybody home out there?"

He leaned back to get a better look at the air hole. "Hello out there, this is me, Chris Palmer."

It was seven o'clock Easter Sunday morning. Chris had just finished running a quarter mile in place — five hundred paces. At least he had *bounced* five hundred paces. It was surprising how tired he felt after jogging in place. It was probably more tiring than actual running would have been, but it was reassuring to feel his legs tingle.

He saw the tiny patch of gray above his air hole. He had hoped to see a ray of sunshine blazing down. Sun meant blue skies and little likelihood of a storm that could dump more snow on him. Anything more than an inch of snow would block his air hole and finish him off.

He wasn't sure what damage a heavy rain would do. Rain would melt off a lot of the snow, but it would also soak him to the skin. And if the weather dropped down to freezing right afterward, which often happened in late winter or early spring, it would probably be the end of him. As long as he kept dry, he could stand the cold.

A tantalizing vision of bacon and eggs suddenly swam before his eyes. Chris groaned with hunger. Then he thought of the grouse. He had to get at that knapsack! He decided to cut the shoulder straps and drag the sack around in front.

Some hard sawing with the hunting knife cut through both straps. After a rest, he tried to pull the sack around his left side. He was able to grab the edge of the bag with his right hand, but his gloved fingers kept sliding off the rough canvas.

He took off the gloves, but his fingers soon grew numb working in the snow. He tried pulling down on the shoulder straps but that only moved the sack higher up on his shoulders. Then he tried to get it even higher, behind his neck. From there he might slide it down over his shoulder. But it went so far and then stuck. No amount of tugging budged it.

Chris went back to pulling the sack around his side. At first he despaired of ever moving it. Then he thought of removing the snow from around it. He dug handfuls of snow from around his left hip, compressed the snow into balls, and shoved them down by his right side.

It took him hours of work and rest, but he finally managed to squeeze the knapsack past his flattened left arm and around in front of his chest. He let it stay, jammed between his chest and the front wall of snow. Afraid that he would never get the buckle undone, he cut the strap, opened the sack, and worked out one of the grouse. Then he maneuvered the knapsack back to his left hip.

He began to pluck the bird. The feathers

would make good insulation against the cold. He stuffed them inside his shirt and down the legs of his pants. Next he opened the bird with his knife and pulled out the guts. Conquering his distaste, he forced himself to eat the heart, the liver, and the kidneys. The rest of the guts, and the head and feet, he put down a hole in the snow near his right knee. He hoped they would freeze and not add to the already foul smell of his cave.

He tore the flesh away from the bones in a sudden burst of appetite. The raw meat almost tasted good. He didn't stop until he had eaten the whole bird. He even broke the bones and sucked out as much of the marrow as he could get. It was rich in the vitamins and minerals he needed.

Chris spent the next hour plucking and cleaning the other two birds. Then, slowly and laboriously, be began to carve out a circular hole in the snow for a refrigerator for his two carcasses.

Digging away, he came across the thick end of a fair-sized branch that had been picked up and carried along in the snow-slide. He tried to carve a hole around the branch, but it ran straight back quite a distance into the snow. He tried to pull it free, but it was stuck fast. Finally he gave up and began to dig in a new place. The excavated snow he packed down into the space between his right hip and the snow wall on that side.

Using his hunting knife as a trowel, he dug and scraped and smoothed a hole large enough to contain the two birds. Then he sealed the hole with a four-inch-deep plug of packed snow. He put the knife back in its scabbard with a feeling of satisfaction. There, his freezer was shut tight for the moment. He could always open it again in a few minutes if he had to.

He dug into the snow and carried a handful to his mouth. The snow melted quickly and he took another couple of handfuls to ease his thirst. The meat probably wouldn't freeze solid, but the cold should slow any spoiling.

He looked up at the air hole. The patch of sky was darker now, but at least it hadn't snowed or rained. Today was Easter Sunday, his third day trapped in the snow. He thought then of his decision to make a calendar. With his finger he drew a line in the snow. He could add a mark every morning. But he realized the snow around him was always changing; the heat of his body tended to melt the skin of the surrounding snow wall. Any marks he made would probably run into each other and become unreadable. He had an idea. He began rummaging around until he found the little pile of bones that remained from his first grouse. He stuck one, two, three bones in a row into the snow at eye level. Now he had a way to keep track of the days. Tomorrow morning he would add another bone. But, please, let someone find him before then.

His legs and feet began to itch again. If there were only some way he could dig down to his ankles and slide his boots out of the skis. Then he might even be able to climb right up and out of the hole. But when he bent forward more than fifteen degrees, his forhead hit the packed snow. He had to be able to bend forward a lot more than that just to reach his knees, not to mention his feet. No, it was hopeless. There was no way he could move that amount of snow. Even if he could, there was no place to put it. Then he had a wild thought. Suppose he just ate the snow? It would pass out of his body as urine, which would melt away even more snow.

Eagerly he began to eat mouthfuls of snow. It didn't take long before he realized the futility of his plan. After the tenth or twelfth mouthful he felt bloated. He couldn't take one more bite of the stuff! When he saw how little space he had cleared, he knew it would take thousands of mouthfuls to make any impression.

He leaned his head back and strained for sounds somewhere up above. The silence was absolute. He had never been in such a quiet place before. It was so quiet that every little sound his body made was magnified a hundred times. After he finished running, his heart pounded like a drum inside his ears. Not only was it deathly quiet, it was also lonely. He had not seen another living thing in two whole days. He couldn't remember, in his entire life, going even one day without seeing another human being.

Suddenly Chris began to laugh. Eat his way out, what a crazy idea! Oh, that was funny all right. Wait till he told everybody about that one!

He laughed and laughed until finally the tears came to his eyes.

# 9

Chris closed his eyes and relived a scene with his mother that had happened years ago.

"You mean no sports of any kind?" he had asked his mother.

"No *competitive* sports," she explained. "Doctor Rickett said you have a heart murmur."

"Aw, Mom, come on!"

Since that conversation, Mom had laid down the law about sports. And there had been something funny about the way his father had started acting. It was as though Dad had agreed to let Mom make the rules for Chris, providing he could make the rules for Terry. So Chris was forbidden to go out for competitive sports while Terry was encouraged. It was really weird.

Chris groaned. It was hard to face the possibility that his parents were acting for their own secret reasons and not for what was best for him and Terry. He hated to think that one of his parents might be using him as a weapon against the other. But why? For what reason?

Chris was sure that his dad loved him. He remembered that during his seige with scarlet fever it was Dad who had slept on a cot in his room every night, who had hovered over his bed every time he cried out in his sleep or woke up in a fevered state. Mom had been there too, of course, bringing him food and changing his sheets and pajamas. It must have been hard on her when he was so sick. She must have been remembering the way they had lost baby Jeanette when she was only ten months old.

Chris rubbed his eyes with his fingertips as though he could wipe out the unhappy memory. It was then that he remembered that he had felt a small hard object in the bottom of the knapsack that he meant to explore when he finished cleaning the grouse. He reached across to his left hip, caught the knapsack and pulled it around in front of him. He tried to peer inside but there wasn't enough light. Taking off his gloves, he rummaged through the sack. Then he felt something round in a hidden inside pocket. His fingers probed a round flat tin, and pushed and prodded the object up out of the pocket.

It was a small compass, practically a toy. He opened the lid and looked inside at the needle. It was furred with rust. The paper compass chart was unreadable and had curled up into the shape of a fortune cookie. The box itself was metal. He vaguely remembered being proud of this compass years ago. He couldn't remember where he had gotten it, but he had used it once to bury some treasure.

He stowed the compass away in the pocket of his jacket. It wasn't any use to him now. What he needed was some way to let people know he was buried in the snow. If only he had a walkie-talkie. There could be dozens of searchers walking all over the slope without being aware that he was just underneath them. If he just had a pole that would stick up above the hole, with maybe a dark piece of cloth tied to the end of it. If he could just get one ski off and get it up where it could be seen. But it would take him forever to work down to his feet. And even if he freed one foot, how could he get the ski loose and work it up past his body and on up through the hole?

He pulled the empty knapsack down over his head. His hood was wet from melted snow, and the canvas sack would offer some protection for his head if a thaw came. It wasn't as hard to breathe inside the sack as he had feared. Of course the light was completely cut off. The dark wasn't cheerful, but he had a feeling that it would not be too bad when he was asleep, or taking a short nap. He would have to keep one hand up near his neck, though, so he could shove the sack up and off his head in case the dome of snow above him suddenly collapsed.

Chris's thoughts drifted back to the compass. If there was only some way to use it. He vaguely remembered sending away for it. Was it a cookie box-top? No, it was fifty cents and three box-tops from a breakfast food. That was before he had had scarlet fever, when he thought he would grow up to be a normal boy — not a kid with a heart murmur. In fact he loved to play baseball and football and basketball. He had not been so bad in those sports either.

He closed his eyes and daydreamed himself into a baseball game. He was on the mound and the score was three to two, their favor. The batter was Terry. Chris had just fired two bullets at his brother, two called strikes. He watched Terry tap the heel of his left shoe with the end of the bat, then step back into the box. Chris reared up and let go. His cap flew off and he came kicking forward off the mound and onto his left leg.

Terry swung all the way around and then had to stab at the ground with his bat to keep from falling on his face. He had been way out in front of the dinky junk curve Chris had fooled him with.

The catcher came running out and jumped at Chris. Then the infield was all around him, pounding him on the back and shaking his hand. As he walked off the field, Terry saluted him with, "You pitched a terrific game there, kid brother."

Chris brought his arm up to check his watch. 12:15. It was time to do a little running again. He decided he would take a nap, with the bag over his head, after the exercises. But in the middle of jogging he rejected the idea of covering up his head. Suppose someone up above was shouting, or calling to him? With the sack over his head he wouldn't hear a thing.

When he finished a quarter mile, he stopped and caught his breath. His legs and feet were all pins and needles again, and he was out of breath and sweating heavily. He still had a tendency to get dizzy when he was running with his eyes open. Something was wrong with his sense of balance. He kept toppling forward.

Then, for the thousandth time since his entrapment, he held his breath and listened for some sound from the outside world. But no matter how hard he strained, he heard nothing except the pounding of his heart.

Discouraged, he dropped his head to his chest and closed his eyes.

Sometime later Chris shivered awake out of his dozing state. He shook his head back and forth, trying to bring some order to his mind. Then he dragged his left arm up to check the time. 6:15. He had slept for almost three hours and he still felt desperately tired. He also had a headache. He could stand anything, though, just so long as he didn't have to go through another siege of diarrhea. The smell from his last attack was finally going away. Either that or he was getting used to it. Could that be where his headache came from, or wasn't he getting any fresh air? He looked up at the air hole. It was still clear. He sighed. What he wouldn't give right now for a bath, just to soak in hot water for a couple of hours.

He reached out for a handful of snow. He was thirsty again. His second handful uncovered the end of the stick that had been in his way when he made the ice-storage hole for the grouse. He had forgotten all about that stick. Could he dig it out? But what good would it do? It was probably less than a foot long. Still, suppose it was longer, long enough to go up through the air hole?

The bark looked smooth and fresh to him, like a piece of green wood. The stick was the thickness of a rake handle, even thicker. It could be a fairly long branch. It might even be long enough to reach up through the air hole.

Chris got out his knife and began to scrape the snow away from the stick. The dug-out snow soon filled up most of the empty space in front of his body. He fumbled the knife back into its sheath, then caught the end of the branch and gave a hard pull. The branch end came toward him an inch or so and then stopped. He pulled harder but no amount of tugging could draw it out any farther.

He decided to push on the branch. It slid back a couple of inches. He pulled forward, pushed back, pulled forward. Perhaps the friction would melt the snow around the branch and loosen it enough so that he could drag it free. He suspected that the branch flared out in a lot of smaller twigs, making it hard to pull free. Nevertheless, he kept up his tug of war. It seemed to him that he was freeing about a quarter of an inch on each push-pull. It encouraged him that the branch was so hard to get loose. It could mean that it was fairly long.

Finally, though, his wrist began to hurt so badly that he had to stop. The awkward angle of the stick imposed a strain on his hand. If the stick had been a foot higher, he could have held it as though he were throwing a spear. A foot lower, and he could have held it as though he were grasping a door knob. But the angle fell in between these two natural positions and forced his hand to work at an artificial stroke. He would have to rest for a while.

Suddenly his head snapped up. What was that, a shout?

He strained his ears and again he heard a faint shout echoing somewhere up above.

Throwing back his head, he began to scream.

# 10

"Hellllllllp! Hellllllllp!" Chris cried over and over.

In between his cries he listened for the sound of an answering shout. Had he imagined those shouts? Was his hearing playing tricks on him? Could it have been the call of a coyote, or even the bark of a bloodhound? After half an hour of shouting and listening, he finally gave up. Closing his eyes he leaned against the wall of snow in front of him. Don't think about it, he told himself, think of something else. But he couldn't. He was cold, hungry, and he stank. A hot meal and a hot bath was all he could think of.

"Somebody find me!" he shouted to the cold and silent snow around him. "Terry, please find me. Mom, Dad, please get me out of here. Please, God, please save me before it's too late."

Then anger overtook him and he reached for the end of the stick and viciously began to jab it back and forth. He wasn't through yet! No, not yet! Not Christopher Palmer! He kept working on the stick until his wrist began to hurt again. But the thick end of the branch was now resting against his chest. After a short break he went back to work. As more of the branch came free, he managed to guide it between the inside of his right arm and his ribs, and down into the snow behind him.

His steady work, interrupted only with brief rests, brought more and more of the branch out of the snow. It also brought him a bonus — a side branch containing four or five tiny maple buds just starting to unfold. He broke off the branch, then snapped off the buds and ate them, ignoring the bitter taste. He was more hopeful than he had been in days. The branch seemed quite long, perhaps long enough to reach above the snow. All he had to do was keep trying to work it free.

Finally he had the branch fully withdrawn, but when he looked up at the air hole, he saw that darkness had fallen. He would have to wait until morning. He put the branch back in its hole. Then he lowered his head to his chest and tried to sleep.

Somehow he got through the night. When daylight finally showed in his air hole, he checked the time. 6:18. And it was Monday morning. He was starting his fourth day of imprisonment. He ate some snow for his thirst, then withdrew the stick from its resting place.

Now came the test. He curved the thin end of the branch up past his head, then pushed the branch up through the loose snow and out the air hole. By raising his arm, he figured he could poke the end of the branch a good two feet above the surface! He even managed, despite his restricted space, to wave the end of the stick. Now if he heard someone calling, he could waggle the branch to attract attention.

He left the stick poking out of the hole, its butt end resting in the snow above his right shoulder. At least he didn't have to worry anymore about a fall of snow cutting off his air supply. Even if the hole did snow over, he could poke it open again. Later he would try to enlarge the hole with the stick to get more air and light, particularly when the sun was shining. If there were only some bright objects he could tie to the end of the branch, some gaily colored piece of rag that would stand out against the snow, even something dark perhaps.

He ate more snow and then remembered that he had not done any running in quite a while. He did not want to forget the exercises, although it seemed to him that there was less and less feeling in his feet and legs. He knew that arm and leg muscles tend to atrophy, to go dead when not in use, but he didn't know how much good his running was doing. His legs and feet felt like big blocks of marble, which meant that his blood circulation was getting worse.

After running in place, he lowered his head to his chest in despair. If he wasn't found in the next day or so, it would be too late. He would probably lose consciousness and then freeze to death. Either that or he would lose his mind. He almost had last night, when he woke up from a dream of playing catch with Terry to live the nightmare of being trapped in the snow — a nightmare that wouldn't go away. He tried desperately to go back to sleep, back to catching Terry's curves and sliders. Would he have to face another endless night? He looked up at the air hole.

Although he wasn't hungry, he decided to dig out one of the grouse and eat some lunch. He had to try to keep up his strength. He got out one of the birds and found that it was still unfrozen. He had expected to have to keep each piece of meat in his mouth for a couple of minutes just to thaw it out.

He tried to stretch out the meal as long as possible. He chewed each scrap of meat fifty times before he swallowed it. Finally he poked the bones away in a hole. Despite his lack of appetite, he finished half a grouse. The other half he put back in storage, then closed up the hole once more with packed snow.

Now what should he do? Spanish words? No, he was fed up with rattling off the days of the week, the months of the year, names, numbers, in Spanish. How about Shakespeare? Or maybe he could try to name all fifty states, and then follow that by naming all the countries in the world. Or should he try to see how many words he could make from the letters in his name. Maybe he should start with something easier — adding up all the numbers. One and two is three and three is six and four is ten and five is fifteen and six is . . .

He got close to a total number of two thousand before he lost track of the whole series. He thought then of his snow calendar. It was Monday morning, his fourth day in the hole. He felt around in his garbage pit for a bone and found one. Then he pressed it into the snow, beside the other three.

He shivered. If worse came to worst, could he use the knife? He shouldn't even think about it. Better think of something else. Spanish. *Bailar*, to dance. *Cantar*, to sing. Go through all the tenses using *cantar* and *bailar* in a sentence. I dance and sing very well. He, she, or it sings and dances very well. *Morir*, to die. I am going to die; he, she, or it is going to die. *Matarse*, to kill oneself. No, don't think of that, think of living, think of dancing and singing. We dance and sing very well. We are not going to die, we are going to sing and dance. I am going to sing and dance.

And thus he held madness at bay through the long afternoon.

# 11

Chris was in a rock cave.

*Crack!* A flash of lightning split the skies outside.

He cowered at the back of the cave. Thunderbolts shattered the heavens, while a heavy rain lashed the earth in solid pounding torrents. Again Chris heard the animal moan.

"No!" he cried out. "Get away!"

The animal entered the cave and padded toward him. Chris threw up his hands to blot out the sight of those ravenous eyes, those fearsome fangs, that red mouth with its lolling tongue and razor sharp teeth. He shrank back against the wet stone.

Suddenly he felt the teeth fasten on his shoulder. He was being dragged out of the cave. He clutched at projecting rocks, but the red coyote easily tore him away.

He was slammed to the ground, all the breath knocked from his body. He lay spread-eagled on his back, looking up at those merciless hot eyes. One front paw gently, delicately, pressed to his chest kept him pinned to the ground. Those gleaming teeth, that open, saliva-spilling mouth came closer and closer. Chris shut his eyes and screamed. He woke up to find himself pushing the end of the branch away from his chest. "No, no," he moaned, still caught in the grip of his nightmare.

Reality came slowly back. It was morning. He leaned back to look up. The air hole was open but there was no sign of the sun. Probably another overcast day. He checked his watch. 9:30. He had slept quite late, though he remembered waking up at least ten times during the night. At one point he must have been hallucinating because he distinctly remembered writing notes and passing them up through the air hole to Mr. Franklin, his science teacher. They were working on a research paper, something to do with taking snow samples. Chris had volunteered to stay in an avalanche for three days.

He pushed the branch away from his chest. If he could keep sawing the branch up and down through the hole, he might enlarge it enough to make sure that another snowstorm could not fill in the opening. Far more of a danger, he knew, would be another snowslide. Another avalanche would sweep his stick away and bury him even deeper under the snow.

Today, Tuesday, for the first time, he felt really weak. Something to eat might help, he decided. He began to dig at the snow to get at the grouse. He took out his knife and carved at the packed snow until the birds were finally uncovered. They were still unfrozen, the flesh still loose and pliable, although the meat was ice cold and hurt his teeth. He finished the other half of the second grouse, cracking all the bones open and sucking them dry. Then he stuck the last bird back in the hole, sealing it away in the hole, sealing it away with a fresh packing of snow. He saved a leg bone as a marker and stuck it beside the other four bones.

"Friday, Saturday, Sunday, Monday, Tuesday," he counted aloud. This was the fifth day in his snow tomb. He didn't think he could last much longer, not the way he was feeling. It required a tremendous effort of concentration to do the simplest thing. He should do some jogging in place, he realized, but he couldn't get up the energy.

He lowered his head and drifted off into a daydream. He was sitting at the kitchen table at home. Opposite him sat a small girl, four or five years old.

"Hi, I'm Jeanette," the little girl said.

"Hi!" Chris answered. He wondered who she was, and what she was doing in their house.

"I'm your big sister."

"Oh," Chris said, confused. His sister, Jeanette, had died before he was born. Anyway, how could she be his big sister when she was obviously smaller than he was?

"You know about me, of course?"

"Sure," Chris answered.

"Momma was very upset."

"Yes, I know." Chris was still confused. His big sister?

"And you're supposed to take my place."

"I am?" Chris said.

"Yes. I don't think it's going to work out very well though."

"Oh?" Chris felt helpless to add anything to the conversation. He didn't know any of the rules for talking to dead sisters.

"Mom and Dad still love me more than they love you."

"That's not true," Chris said, though he suspected that she might be right.

"Oh, yes, there will never be another Jeanette as far as Mom and Dad are concerned. You must be a big disappointment to them," she said, "after Terry and me. Poor Prissy-Chrissy!"

"Don't call me that," he shouted.

"Prissy-Chrissy!" she shouted. "Prissy-Chrissy! Prissy-Chrissy!"

He came floating back to reality with the sound of that hated nickname in his ears. He had been called that for a while in the fifth and sixth grades, especially by one kid who, fortunately, had moved out of town after sixth-grade graduation. Thankfully, no one remembered the name now. Still he shivered. What a weird and terrible dream! What a strange thing to come out of his mind.

Chris thought back on all that he had heard about his sister's death. Crib Death, the doctors called it. Nobody seemed to know what caused it, but it sometimes happened to babies under the age of one year.

One evening Mom and Dad were watching television in the living room. About five minutes to ten, Mom thought she heard the baby cry out and asked Dad to go up and look in on her. Dad said that Mom was imagining things, but he would check as soon as the program was over.

But when the program was over, the news, with pictures of devastating floods in the Midwest, came on and they forgot about the baby's cry. When they went upstairs to go to bed an hour later, Mom looked in on Jeanette. The baby wasn't breathing.

When they talked with Doctor Rickett at the hospital later, he said the baby had been dead for at least two hours when they brought her in at 11:30. So Mom couldn't have heard that cry from upstairs around 10 o'clock. And wouldn't the cry have awakened Terry, who was sleeping in the same room?

That was the story, as well as Chris could piece it together from remarks he had heard over the years. Yet there was no question that Mom still blamed Dad for not checking on the baby that night — even though, from all Chris knew, it would have been too late anyway.

Poor Mom, Chris thought, she must have been crazy with grief, and with blaming herself for not going up to answer Jeanette when she thought she heard that cry. The reason she blamed Dad was because she couldn't bear to keep on blaming herself. And poor Dad, he must have felt guilty too. He must have wished over and over that he had gone up when Mom had asked him to.

Still thinking of his baby sister, Chris pushed the branch up above the top of the hole and tried to wriggle it around a bit. It was funny, he thought, but he had never heard Mom and Dad talk about Jeanette's death. All of his information had come from other relatives or friends. Once he heard Aunt Eileen and Uncle Phil talking about the baby. Another time old Bo Packer, who worked at times for the Palmers as a handyman, told Chris what he knew about his sister's death. Her death *must* be the reason Mom was so careful with his health. He was a replacement for

Jeanette, and Mom wasn't going to let any harm come to him if she could help it.

For a moment Chris felt a wave of suspicion. Could his mother have invented the return of that heart murmur to give her an excuse to protect him? After all, he had only her word for it.

Chris suddenly realized with a shock of discovery that he was constantly trying to prove to himself that Mom and Dad loved him more than they loved Terry. And that he did this because deep down he doubted that Mom and Dad really did love him. He had come to feel that he was a replacement for Jeanette and not a person in his own right.

A shiver passed over him. How mixed-up their lives were! It seemed to him that he had learned more about himself in the few days that he had been trapped in the snow than in all the rest of his life put together. Of course all he could do now was think about his life, but it was something he had done very little of before. It seemed as though all he had been doing with his life was going along, just letting things happen to him. He had let others always decide what was best for him. Maybe they were right, but that wasn't the point. He should control his own life. He had a right to be consulted, to make his own mistakes.

Then anger at his plight overtook him. Was he going to lose his life just when he was beginning to understand it?

# 12

"Here it comes!" someone shouted. The rope dangled in front of Chris.

"Tie it around your chest, under your shoulders," the voice shouted down.

Chris tried to work the rope around behind his back.

"It's no use," someone said. "This one is done for. He doesn't answer."

Chris screamed. "It's me, Chris Palmer. I'm alive! *Yo soy*, Chris Palmer," he repeated in Spanish.

The conversation continued somewhere above him. "Young fellows nowadays have no stamina."

"You're right. Let's pull up the rope. If we hurry, we can still get in a few rounds of golf."

Chris grabbed the rope and hung on. He mustn't let them get away!

When he woke up he was gripping the branch so tightly with his right hand that his fingers ached. For a moment he was lost, then the whole horror of his situation came back to him once again. Automatically he looked up to check the air hole. It was still open.

He checked his watch. Almost noon. But what day was it? Five bones were in the snow right there in front of him. Friday, Saturday, Sunday, Monday, Tuesday, he counted. His tongue ran over his teeth and he felt the fur clinging to them. He had not brushed his teeth since Friday. Slowly, wearily, he got the mitten and glove off his right hand, then dug out a finger of snow and used it to brush his teeth. He ran his forefinger back and forth over the front teeth and as many of the back teeth as he could reach. He spat out. Then he cupped a handful of snow and washed his face with it. His cheeks stung when he was finished. A shiver ran over him. He got the glove and mitten back on, then began to run in place. He would do five hundred paces.

While he was running, he thought how unfair he had been to Terry. He had always tried to put him down, had treated him as a rival for their parents' love. From now on he would be a lot nicer to Terry, he would let him know how much he had always secretly admired him.

To start making it up to his brother, in the only way he could at the moment, Chris replayed an earlier daydream. He toed the rubber, checked the runners at first and third, nodded at the catcher's sign, then reared back and let go with his fast ball. Terry timed the swing perfectly. His brother's shoulders went taut with the shock of bat-meeting-ball. Chris did not even turn around. He knew that one was gone. Terry's teammates erupted from the bench and crowded around home plate. When Chris came trudging off the mound, he nodded to his brother and said, "You're really something, you know that, don't you?"

Terry grinned. "A lucky swing, that's all."

Then Chris was overcome with rage again. "Help!" He threw back his head and roared the word over and over again.

But silence was his only answer. In a few minutes he gave up shouting. Losing his head wasn't going to help. He should try to figure out some way to attach a bright object to the end of the stick, something that would attract attention. Could he rip a sleeve off his shirt? Or use his T-shirt? But they were white and would not stand out against the snow. He really had nothing, let's face it. He decided to dig out the remaining grouse and pick some meat off the bones. Now he was on the last of his food. Either someone would find him soon or he would die from exposure. This was his fifth day in his snow prison, and he doubted if he could last more than another twenty-four hours.

He held the grouse in his gloved hands and pulled the flesh off the bones with his teeth. The bird was too cold to eat with his bare fingers. He had tried but the cold made them so stiff and clumsy that he had to put the gloves back on.

He finished half the grouse and felt a little better. The splintered bones he pushed down into the hole near his right knee that he now called his garbage pit. It probably made no difference if he rationed his food. It only had so many calories, right? Rationing wouldn't add a single calorie; in fact he might even lose some food value by holding on to the meat too long. One good thing at least, that awful bout of diarrhea had not come back.

He packed snow into the hole, sealing away his last half grouse. Then he put the knife back in its sheath and reached up for the branch. He twirled and waved it for as long as he could. If there were only some leaves on the end of it. But if there were leaves, it would be summer and he wouldn't be caught in a snowslide.

For the hundredth time he wondered how Mom and Dad were taking his disappearance. They would blame themselves, and each other, for letting him go out that morning. Mom would feel that she should not have let him go cross-country skiing by himself. And Dad would blame himself because he had heard the weather report and knew that snow was predicted. He would also blame himself because he had not warned Chris to be on the lookout for avalanches. Wow, he simply *had* to survive! He couldn't put his parents through another experience like Jeanette! And he didn't want to leave Terry alone with his parents, either.

He suddenly felt that he was on the verge of some tremendous truth about himself. He was blindly stumbling his way through emotions and feelings he had kept hidden for years — hatred and envy and shame — that he had bottled up.

"Terry! Terry!" he called out.

But all he heard was the deafening quiet of his snow tomb.

"Terry, you've got to find me!" Chris shouted. "There are so many things we have to straighten out!"

# 13

"It's very simple," the animal said.

Chris was twelve years old again and having breakfast at home. Across the table sat the red coyote.

"You see," the coyote was saying, "I have a baby quota to meet."

"Is it large?" Chris asked.

"Oh yes, quite large. However, I *can* tell you that baby Jeanette never felt a thing." The animal raised one paw to show Chris.

"Oh?"

"I placed this paw gently over her mouth," the coyote said. "I am quite expert at this sort of thing."

"Oh, I don't think you're real," Chris said, shaking a spoonful of sugar over his cereal.

The coyote laughed. "Oh yes, many people try to deny me. But it's no use. You and I, for example, have an appointment in a few years." The coyote lifted the cereal box. "May I join you?"

"Sure, help yourself."

Chris stared at the picture of a small black compass on the outside of the box. "Get your forest survival kit," he read. "Secret mirror in back of compass can be used to start campfires and send coded signals. Send one dollar and three box-tops from this package to . . ."

Chris reached for the box. He would send away for the compass. He could put it in his knapsack and take it everywhere with him, along with his fold-up trenching shovel, his canteen, and his snap-lid ammo box from World War II.

Suddenly the coyote jumped down from the chair, ran out the back door, and bounded away up the mountain behind their house.

Chris ran after him. "Hey wait!" he called as he stumbled over buckets and rakes in the back yard.

He woke up struggling in his snow prison and felt the usual deep outrage on discovering that he was still trapped. That was the worst thing about waking up, that awful despair on finding out that he was still caught in the snow. He looked up to check his air hole. Still dark outside.

He closed his eyes again and let his thoughts drift back to the dream. It was funny, but he instantly recognized that cereal box, although he had not eaten "Bran-New" flakes in years. He could still remember the day he wheedled a dollar out of his mother to send away for the compass. And there had been a secret mirror too. Funny he hadn't remembered that until just now. The mirror was probably lost years ago. Wait a minute, it was part of the compass lid — it might still be there!

His eyes flew open and eagerly he reached for the empty knapsack. In a minute he had his gloves off, the compass out, and was turning it over in his hands. Inside the hinged cover, wasn't that where it was? Wasn't it part of the lid? Careful now, he cautioned himself. *Don't drop it!* He opened the stiff cover and felt the inside of the case. But how did the mirror come out? There was some trick to it.

It wasn't so much his mind as his fingers that remembered how to get at the mirror. His thumb and forefinger were pressing on the outside of the lid and suddenly a circular piece of metal popped loose from the inside of the lid. Excited now, he rubbed the thin metal disc back and forth on the wool of his sweater. Although it was almost pitch black in the snow hole, he could faintly see a ring of brightness in front of him.

If his memory was right, then one side of the mirror was painted jungle green and the other side was polished to a brilliant shine.

He put the mirror away in his shirt pocket, and replaced the compass in the knapsack. He shoved the canvas sack to one side. He had to figure out some way to use the mirror. Could he tie it to the end of the branch and then poke it out through the hole?

He watched the air hole for what seemed like hours before dawn finally came, before one side of the snow around the hole turned a deep orange, then faded to a light pink as the sun rose higher in the sky. It was going to be a sunny day!

Excited now, he lowered the branch, poking it down into the snow between his legs until the tip of the branch was opposite his face. Now he had to attach the mirror to the end of the stick.

He pulled his gloves off with his teeth, then reached around for the knapsack. One look at the straps told him that they would not work. They were too bulky; they would cover up the mirror. If he could only get at his bootlaces!

He tried to bend forward but it was hopeless. Then he tried once again to squat, but his body became jammed against the snow and he could not lower himself. The snow itself seemed to have changed. It was more icy, more grainy, where before it had been powdery. He felt the temperature in his snow hole getting colder as the snow became more ice-like.

Did he have to give up on the idea of tying the mirror to the end of the stick? No, but first he'd eat. It was morning, time to mark another day on his calendar. He rummaged in his garbage pit until he found a bone, then stuck it in the snow along with the others. Now his calendar was a little face: two ends of bones for the eyes, a short bone for the nose, a bone pressed in sideways for the mouth, and one bone for each ear — his Mister Snowtime. And what day did Mister Snowtime say it was? Wednesday.

He dragged his left arm up to check the time. 10:05. It had been around two p.m., Friday, when the avalanche tore loose. This was Wednesday. He had been trapped Friday afternoon, or five complete days at two p.m. today — five days or one hundred and twenty hours. He would count on being rescued before six complete days had gone by, either rescued or out of his misery. That meant a total of one hundred and forty-four hours. He had to endure the cold and the dark and the loneliness for another twenty-eight hours. Surely he could hang on for that long.

He was afraid the snow might damage his watch. So he took it off and put it in his shirt pocket. It was safer there.

Then he heard a sound that electrified him; the whimpering of a dog!

# 14

The thin nose poked into the hole, blocking out the sunlight. Looking up, all Chris saw was the black button of a dog's nose.

"That's a good boy, good dog," he called. "Now bark!"

The nose withdrew and a small paw passed over the hole. Now Chris could see the underside of the animal. The leg was slender, almost delicate, and the white grizzled fur hung down in long matted clots. The animal wheeled in excitement and Chris caught a glimpse of gaunt ribs and a bushy tail.

"Coyote," he groaned in disgust. "Another coyote!"

Paws began to scratch at the crusted snow around the hole.

"Go away. *Scat!*" Chris screamed, suddenly afraid that the animal's digging would cause the whole snow dome to collapse down around his head. Then he thought of the stick. He raised it up and jabbed it through the hole with all his might.

There was a startled yelp. He must have hit the animal somewhere on the face. There was a final puzzled whimper, a last retreating whisper of paws over ice. Then nothing more to be seen or heard.

Chris waited. The minutes passed. Finally he accepted the fact that the animal had gone. It was a male, probably out foraging for his mate and her hungry brood. Spring was the worst time of the year for them, he knew. The hungriest time. Thank God the animal hadn't decided to dig down to him, and thank God again for the branch. Then disappointment flooded over him. He had been sure that someone had discovered him, sure that someone's dog had finally located him.

Anger followed quickly on the disappointment and he cried out, "But it's not fair! It's not fair!"

In a sudden fury Chris brought up his fists and hammered at the snow in front of him. "How about my heart now, Mom? Is this bad for my heart?" Everybody was leading his life for him and he had to practically lose his life to find that out.

Suddenly he did something that astonished him — he burst into tears. They went on and on. He just couldn't stop them. Every time he thought the crying jag was over, it started up again. Sob after racking sob seemed to come up from the very pit of his stomach. He cried so long and so hard that his stomach muscles hurt. He could feel tears coursing down his cheeks, then running along his neck and inside his shirt. He never did control the crying. It was pain and exhaustion that finally forced him to stop. For a long time he hung limp, held up by the snow, his chin resting on his chest.

When he finally came out of it, he had changed. He felt calm, peaceful. The thought of death no longer frightened him. He accepted the fact that he would probably die — by his own hand if necessary. In the meantime, he would do whatever he could to make possible his rescue. For whatever few days, or hours, were left to him, he was going to conduct himself with as much courage as he could muster. When they found his body, they would also find evidence to show that he had tried to free himself, right up to the very end.

Now he had to do something with that mirror. He got off his right glove and reached inside his jacket and sweater to get at his shirt pocket. He snagged a fingernail on the sweater and he had to patiently work a piece of wool out of his split nail. *That was it!* He could use the wool in his sweater, or even one of his gloves. He could unravel a strand and tie the mirror to the stick with it. As it happened, Mom had knitted the sweater for him. And because the sweater had been hand knit, it would be easy to tease a strand of wool from it.

He pulled out the compass mirror and held the shiny side up to his face. Despite the dim light he could make out his features. He was shocked by his appearance. There were large black patches under his eyes and his cheeks had a sunken look. His lips were blue and his whole face was streaked with dirt. How did he get so dirty?

He rubbed the mirror on his sweater to

clean it, then put it in his jacket pocket for the moment. First he had to fix the stick. He lowered the branch down into the slot beside his right leg. The end of the branch was too thin, too weak, to hold the mirror. He would have to take off the top twelve inches or so. Fortunately that still left enough to show above the surface.

He broke the branch. Because the wood was green it split lengthwise, instead of breaking cleanly in two, and he had to use his knife to trim off the split end. The blade of his knife was dull and it took ten minutes of patient sawing to cut through the green wood.

The tip, though noticeably thicker now, was split in two for the first three inches of its length. Chris wondered if he could stick the round mirror halfway into the split, then bind up the halves of the branch tip with the wool from his sweater.

He reached inside his jacket, teased out a strand of wool from the sweater and began to pull on it. When it was long enough, he slipped the knife under the strand and cut the wool. The knitting unraveled easily and soon he had a piece of wool about two feet long.

He propped the branch in the snow so

that his hands would be free to work. He stuck the mirror into the split, then began to wrap the wool around the branch to hold the split ends together. Despite his numb fingers, he made sure the strand of wool was as tight as he could get it. After a brief rest to warm his fingers, he finished wrapping the tip. Then he triple-tied the strand of wool and tested his work. The mirror held firm. Though part of its surface was covered, there was enough mirror showing to flash plenty of sunlight.

He poked the branch gently through the hole. A half twist and he could see the bright image of the sun exploding off the polished metal. Grains of ice adhered to the surface of the mirror but they would soon melt off, he knew. He turned the stick completely around until the sun hit it again. He decided to rotate the mirror about a quarter turn each way, enough to make sure that the sun flashed fully off the polished surface.

As long as he had sunshine he would continue to twirl the branch. It required very little effort and the more he flashed the mirror, the more likely it was that someone would spot it.

He left the mirror sticking up above the hole and checked his watch. It was almost 2:00 p.m. He had now survived five full days of imprisonment. One hundred twenty hours.

Surely he could last one more day!

# 15

To pass the time that night, Chris decided to paint the bedroom he shared with Terry. And of course he let Terry boss the job.

"Okay, get a screwdriver," Terry told him. "Take the switch and outlet plates off. I'll go get the spackle and patch those cracks in the ceiling."

"Yes, sir, boss," Chris said, with the usual joking sarcasm he used when Terry was giving him an order.

Chris got the drop cloths out of the basement, then spread them over the floor. He could almost read the family history of the past five years in those old sheets. There were the white drops from the outside windows on the south side of the house; the gray spots from the porch ceiling two summers ago; a scattering of very fine green drops from last year, when he and Dad had roller painted the downstairs hallway an avocado green; and there was the red outline of a bicycle frame — Chris's five-speed.

Chris spread the old sheets over the floor, working them right into the corners. He and Terry painted steadily for a couple of hours. The four windows took fifteen minutes each. Chris did the old-fashioned cast-iron radiator, and Terry the door and closet frames.

Terry was folding the drop cloths and Chris was washing off the rollers and the cut-in brushes when a faint ray of light began to brighten the gloom in the snow hole.

"Guess we're about finished," Chris said as Terry faded away with a final wave of his hand.

Chris looked up at his air hole, now visible as a pale circle of light above him. "Welcome, Thursday," he said thankfully.

Nighttime gave him the horrors. At night he was blind as well as trapped.

He lowered his head, then rummaged around looking for another bit of bone. He found one and stuck it in his Mister Snowtime face, adding a new bone to the mouth, which now tilted upward in a smile. Next he inspected his mirror, rubbing frost off the metal with the neck edge of his sweater. He raised the branch through the hole and revolved it several times. There was no sign of the sun.

Although there seemed to be no feeling left in his lower limbs, he tried to run in place. He thought of Terry and turned the running into a form of competition. If he were rescued maybe he could get his name in the *Guinness Book of World Records*. Chris smiled to himself at the thought. That was one heck of a competition all right — avalanche survival. Almost as ridiculous as the one he and Terry had spent one whole afternoon arguing about: which one of them could walk in and out of the Snake River Canyon the fastest.

After a few minutes Chris stopped running and took his watch out of his shirt pocket. He pressed the time button — 6:15. It had to be more than that! Time had a way of playing tricks on him. He would close his eyes to doze for a few minutes, then wake up to discover that he had slept for two hours. Or he would daydream for what seemed like hours, only to find out that his daydream had lasted just a few minutes.

He glanced up at the air hole. The sun had finally come up! Raising his arm, he revolved the branch a quarter turn, watching the sun grow, explode, and die in the shiny metal. Every minute or so he would stop twirling the branch to listen as hard as he could. But the only thing he heard was the lonely whisper of the wind sweeping across the snow.

When he grew tired of twirling the branch, he stuck the butt end in the snow at such an angle that the sun continued to bounce off the face of the mirror. Suddenly ravenous with hunger, he unpacked the snow from the front of his refrigerator. Even before the white wrinkled meat came into view, he recoiled from the smell. The meat had turned bad. He found that he could not touch any of the flesh. He pushed it deeper into the hole and covered it again with snow. If he got desperate enough, he might tackle it later in the afternoon.

To give his stomach muscles something to work on, he cut away a few slices of snow and let them melt in his mouth. He was careful not to eat too much snow as he feared getting diarrhea again.

After that he thought of the leather knapsack straps and pulled the bag around. With his hunting knife, he cut off an inch of strap and began to chew on it. There were probably no calories left in the leather, and the taste was harsh, but it felt good to be chewing on something again.

This was his seventh consecutive day, he reflected. Had anyone ever survived that long, buried alive in snow? Of course he would have to be rescued before he could claim a record. He would send a letter to the *Guinness Book of World Records*. Longest time trapped in the snow, maybe? Longest trapped underground? An entry in this book was the least he was entitled to. He would make sure that he wasn't cheated out of the recognition due him.

With an entry in the *Guinness Book of Records*, he ought to get a full four-year college scholarship somewhere! There would be a victory parade for him, and he would be presented to the Governor of Idaho.

He came out of this dream to find himself in total darkness. Some dream. Talk about wishful thinking. But why was it so dark? For a moment he feared that the snow dome had collapsed on him. Then he realized that the hood of his jacket had fallen down over his head. He pushed the hood back and looked up. He revolved the stick a few times to see where the sun was and noted its bouncing reflections off the metal mirror. It was afternoon. He checked the time again: 4:30. He felt strangely lightheaded and began to sing, "Farmer In The Dell." It seemed important to sing as loudly as he could and to sing the song all the way through to the "cheese stands alone." Singing the song was part of the competition. They were making it as hard as they could on him. He had to see someone about that, to make an official protest.

As soon as he stopped singing he became

convinced that he was upside down in the snow. Maybe it was better that way, he decided. His rescuers could pull off his skis, then tie a rope to his legs and haul him out. Then he could claim a record for being buried upside down in the snow. No, that was all wrong. He was writing to the Governor of Idaho about the *Guinness Book of Records*, how they wouldn't list him as a record holder. There was the Governor now, and he was laughing at him!

Chris's head jerked up as he stared into the grinning face of Mister Snowtime. He lashed out with his fist. He would beat the Governor's face to a pulp. He would beat anyone who tried to cheat him of his record! But his blows were mushy soft and his fists merely pushed the bones deeper into the snow.

As Chris made it halfway back to reality, he looked into the battered face of the Governor and realized that he had only messed up his snow calendar. Now he wouldn't be able to tell what day it was. He wouldn't know if he broke the record. He wouldn't know! He wouldn't know! He burst into tears. He couldn't take any more. He couldn't take another night of the cold, another night of the dark, of the pain, of loneliness.

Dear God, he prayed, end it all tonight, please? Christopher Palmer doesn't want to live here anymore.

# 16

It was Friday. Teams of rescuers had been looking for Chris without success. Even so, his father was now preparing for another day's search. He stood on the front bumper of a La France fire truck in the Salmon Springs firehouse.

"Okay, everybody, your attention please!" Jack Palmer said.

The conversation died down as the knots of men in the firehouse fell silent. Most were drinking coffee from paper mugs, or smoking cigarettes.

"We've covered all the slopes between my house and Frenchman's Flats. We've found three small slides and probed two of them thoroughly. The Forest Service crew is going to finish working over the third one, the Cougar Creek site, today."

Terry Palmer looked up at his father. He was shocked at the change in his face. The older man looked as if he had lost twenty pounds. But it was the eyes that bothered Terry the most. They had a flat, dead look, as though Jack Palmer was convinced he would never see his younger son alive again.

"Fire companies one and two are going to work the territory south of the Flats and toward Turkey Meadows. As usual, we're splitting the highway department into two crews. They're assembling right now at the highway barn."

"Jack?"

"Yes." Jack Palmer looked down at the speaker.

"There's no chance that kid of yours did something crazy, like leave home without telling anyone?"

Jack Palmer shook his head. "No, no way."

"Didn't he run away from home once before, when he was thirteen or fourteen?"

Terry Palmer felt a stab of pity for his father. Terry didn't know how the rumor had gotten started, but some people were now saying that Chris had run away from home. Another rumor had it that Chris was seen in Lewistown on Easter Sunday. And to top it off, there was yet another rumor going around that Chris had run away from home for three or four days when he was only twelve.

"I've already answered that," Jack Palmer was saying. "Chris has never left home in his life before, for any reason."

"Go ahead, Jack," someone shouted.

"Right. I want to thank everyone for turning out again. I know the chances are getting slim and that you all have your own jobs and businesses to get back to. But I want you all to know that I appreciate what you've been doing to help. My family and I won't ever forget you for this."

For a moment it looked as though Jack Palmer was going to break down. His shoulders suddenly hunched forward and his voice broke.

Someone from the crowd took charge. "Okay guys, let's go! It'll be light by the time we hit the slopes."

The men began moving out of the firehouse and over to their cars and trucks in the parking lot.

Finally Jack Palmer joined his son. Father and son had been working twenty-hour days since Chris had failed to return home. They were now exhausted.

"Okay, Terry, I'll take my highway crew again, and you go with Granger's crew."

"Dad, I wanted to talk to you," Terry said.

"Yes?"

Jack Palmer reached his pickup, stopped, and turned around to face his son.

"When we were having breakfast this morning I kept thinking of an argument I had with Chris a couple of months ago."

"Get in," Jack Palmer said.

"We were arguing, Chris and I, about the Snake River Canyon," Terry said, slamming the door. "It was a dumb argument. Chris was saying that he could walk down into the canyon, and back up again, faster than I could."

"So?" The engine of the pickup rumbled to life. Soon they were driving through the still dark streets of Salmon Springs. Terry noticed a light upstairs in the Mayberry house. Old Mrs. Mayberry was very sick, and not expected to live much longer. She had nurses around the clock. For a moment Terry wondered if she could hear the sound of their pickup, and what it meant to her. Then he shivered. Death was something he didn't want to think about right now.

"Well, Dad, he got really hot about it. He really believed he could."

"Well, maybe he could."

"Come on, Dad. You know he doesn't have the stamina I have."

"Stamina's not everything."

"Okay, but anyway here's what I think. He wanted to do something to show he was tougher than I am. I think he may have tried to ski into Hidden Lake."

"Look, we've been over this before," Jack Palmer said. "The army copter from Fort Green flew over that area on Sunday. They reported no sign of any tracks, no sign of an avalanche, or anything out of the ordinary."

"I know, Dad, but Saturday night's snowstorm must have wiped out his tracks. And anyway, it's not all that easy to spot a snowslide — even from the air."

"That may be, but I'm not playing

hunches. The most logical thing to assume is that he dropped down into the lower slopes from Frenchman's Flats. He was more likely to find game in that direction than up around Hidden Lake."

"I know all that, Dad, but I still think he tried Hidden Lake. Imagine what a big deal it would have been for him to come back and tell us that he skied into Hidden Lake."

"I don't think he would have done it," Jack Palmer said. "Not with snow forecast that day."

"Wasn't it just a *chance* of snow?" Terry asked.

"Okay, scattered snow showers, but he still wouldn't have tried to reach Hidden Lake. Maybe *you* would have, but not Chris. He's too cautious."

"But, Dad," Terry argued. "You don't know him like I do."

"I don't know my own son! Is that what you're saying?"

Terry gave up. What was the use? His father just couldn't understand. But the problem with doing everything in a methodical and logical way was that Chris just didn't have the time. If he were trapped somewhere, lying somewhere with a broken leg, he couldn't last much longer. Already it might be too late. But what could he do? His father's mind was made up.

The pickup rolled through the wide open gates of the highway department compound, then past a line of yellow road graders and front-end loaders. It slowed to a stop in front of the highway barn.

Ted Granger detached himself from a knot of men and came toward the truck.

Jack Palmer cut the engine and turned to look at Terry.

"You go with Granger and that's it."

"Okay, Dad. Okay."

While his father and Ted Granger went over their plans, Terry went into the highway barn and stretched out on a stack of peat moss bales. It would take another half hour to get everything organized. In the meantime he would catch a catnap.

He curled up, laid his head on his arm, and dropped right off to sleep.

# 17

"It's closing in, I know it is!" Chris patted the snow wall. Though he could barely see in the dim light, he had the distinct impression that the walls of his snow tomb were closing in.

He looked up at the barely visible dark blue hole above his head. It now seemed much closer. Was the whole snow dome slowly settling down around him? It was impossible to tell in the dark. It seemed like it, though. Was that a star?

His legs began to itch again and he moaned. He tried to ripple the skin to make the itch go away. Had he lost enough weight to slide his feet right out of his boots? Surely they were thin enough to come out. He tugged and got nowhere. He wasn't even sure he had moved his feet. There was no feeling left down there.

One thing, though, he wasn't going to look up now. The red coyote was up there, waiting for him. He was up there gloating. As soon as Chris died, the coyote would slip down the hole and tear apart his still warm body. But Chris Palmer wasn't dead yet!

Back to Spanish verbs. Do some Shakespeare. Do some arithmetic. Eeny meeny miney mo, who will save me from the snow? If I die before I wake, to God in heaven my soul to take.

As the night faded and light gradually infiltrated his surroundings, Chris knew that this had to be his last day. He was now so weak it required a tremendous effort of will just to raise his arm. He thought his legs were frozen beyond any hope of thawing out. Even if he were rescued it would probably be too late to save them. And who wanted to live like that? If Mom thought it was bad having a heart murmur, what would she think if he had no legs? Or no hands?

He looked up at the air hole. If there were no sun today, then his chances were zero. He might last through the day, but he wasn't going to go through another night. A plan had been forming in his mind. He had found a way out but he had to act before he was helpless.

Painfully he forced himself to push the branch up until the mirror was clear of the surface. He revolved the stick a couple of times, but could not see any light flashing off the polished side of the disc.

Perhaps it was too early. He lowered the branch and reached inside his sweater to his shirt pocket. His fingers were almost helpless and he had to take out the watch by cupping it in his palm. He got the watch up in front of his face and read the time with a sinking feeling in his stomach: 7:45. The sun had risen by now. Again he glanced up at the mirror — there was no sign of any sunshine, which meant that the day was overcast. He would have to keep checking, though; it could be partially cloudy. He could not afford to miss any clear periods of sunshine. And today was Friday, wasn't it? Already it was a week.

He groaned. What was the use? He was doomed. Anyway, they would look everywhere for him except in the direction of Hidden Lake. He was a good five miles from Frenchman's Flats. Who would ever suspect, on a cold March day, with snow forecast, that he would head into the high mountains? He was going to die. And it was all due to his stupidity.

He started to check the time again. Maybe the date and month part was working now. As he took the watch out of his pocket, it slipped from his lifeless fingers. He made a grab for it and missed. He looked around dully for the wristwatch. Then he spotted it. The watch had slid down to his right knee. What was the use? What did he need a watch for? His time had run out — all his hours were used up.

Nevertheless, he tried to reach the watch. By digging his right shoulder into the snow, and pressing down as hard as he could, he was just able to touch the end of the strap. But he had to be very careful. There was about an inch clearance all the way around his right leg, around both legs.

If he were not careful, the watch would slide on down and fall permanently out of reach.

He couldn't see where his fingers were groping. Scrunched down the way he was, his face was thrust forward into the snow wall. And to make matters worse, he had almost no feeling in his fingers.

He patted around, following his right leg downward. At first he felt nothing. Then he sensed an object, cupped it in his hand, and straightened up. His numb blue fingers were gripping a piece of frozen snow. He dropped the snow and looked down.

The watch was no longer visible, but he saw the strap buckle down at his ankle. He stared at the barely visible strap end. The watch had been like a friend, a companion. It had a life of its own and flashed the time in colorful red numbers. The watch had been a Christmas present from his father. It spoke of a safe, warm, orderly world full of love and color and kindness, where terrible things were not allowed to happen. Now it was gone. He had lost his final link with the outside world. Gone, too, were Mom and Dad and Terry — nothing or no one could save him now. It was all over. His time was up.

In a sudden fury he began rocking the upper half of his body back and forth, as though straining against chains that were binding him.

"Give out, heart!" he cried. "Give out and finish me!" Then he threw back his head and howled. "Help me! Help me! Help me, somebody!"

Something crossed his air hole, dimming the light in his tomb. He strained his head back. A large black object, an animal of some kind, was pawing at the hole. The red coyote had finally come for him. And just in time too. Christopher Palmer was ready. But what was the animal doing to the mirror?

Those black shadowy movements separated, and distinct shapes came into focus —a wing, a feathered body, a stick leg. Chris found himself looking at a large black bird with a yellow beak.

The bird was attacking the mirror. Chris heard the *ping* of beak meeting metal. The bird was working at the woolen strand! The mirror and branch swung completely around and Chris saw a flash of sunlight. The bird was nest building, he realized, and probably wouldn't stop until it had unraveled all the wool and loosened the mirror.

In a rage he screamed up at the bird: "*Yaah! Go away!*"

The black body lifted. Chris spotted a white patch on the wings and recognized the intruder as a magpie. A childhood rhyme came to his lips, something you said when you saw magpies. "One for sorrow," he whispered, "two for joy, three for a girl, and four for a boy."

Yes, that was it, he decided, one for sorrow. He finally had the message. His head snapped forward and he passed out.

Terry Palmer sat up suddenly on the bale of peat moss. What had happened? Where was everyone? He scrambled down from the pile of bales and ran outside the highway barn. Where had everybody gone?

Someone was gassing up a dump truck at the shed off to one side of the barn. He trotted over and recognized Luther Curry, one of the highway workers.

"Where did everybody go?" he asked.

"They're all out searching for your brother."

"Why didn't they call me?"

"Granger said you looked so bushed he didn't have the heart to wake you up."

"But I want to be out there with everybody else."

"Take it easy. You're not going to do anyone any good if you collapse from exhaustion." Luther hung up the hose and put the cap back on the gas tank. "Anyway, somebody will be here at lunchtime. You can go back out then."

"What time is it now?"

"Around nine."

"You mean I slept for two hours?"

"Yes, just about."

"Where are *you* going?" Terry asked.

"I gotta pick up a compressor we left out overnight."

"Are you going anywhere near my home?"

"Sort of. You want a lift?"

"Yeah."

Fifteen minutes later Terry was sneaking around the back of his house. He did not want to meet his mother, not right now. She would try to stop him if she knew he was going to Hidden Lake. Or she would insist on someone going with him, and he had no time for that right now.

He slipped into the barn. He would take his father's firefighter's field pack. It had a medical kit, rope, canned food, a fold-up trenching shovel, a flashlight, and other emergency supplies. He got the pack on his shoulders. What else could he use? Flares to send up a signal. There were flares in the jeep. His father never traveled anywhere without them. He took a half dozen flares from the jeep and shoved them in his pack. Then he got into his skis. He looked over at the back door of the kitchen, didn't see his mother, then skied out around by the back of the barn and picked up the trail for Frenchman's Flats.

If he was lucky, he thought, he would find Chris lying somewhere with a broken leg. If he wasn't lucky — but he wouldn't think about that.

Tears sprang to Terry's eyes and he wiped them away with the back of his hand. They had to find Chris. Mom was nearly out of her head and Dad had aged ten years in the past week. Also, Terry wanted, needed, his brainy kid brother. He shook his head, angry with himself. Crying wasn't going to do any good; he had to keep his mind on what he was doing.

A mile on the other side of Frenchman's Flats he came to a long open slope and stopped. He shaded his eyes and looked down the incline. There was a curious, large snow-covered mound at the bottom of the slope, but that was probably rubble from a summer landslide. A magpie lifted from the mound and flapped away. Terry looked up at the sky, at the broken patches of cloud, then stabbed the snow with his poles and urged himself forward.

As he skied on, his eyes kept scanning the land ahead and on each side, looking for a dark black bundle against the snow. He turned to check the lower slope, and picked up the magpie again. It was dropping down to the snow. He watched the bird land, fold its wings, and jauntily step around. The head bent to peck at something, and a stabbing flash of light winked out. Terry coasted to a stop. It was probably nothing, a trick of light, the sun bouncing off a patch of glare ice. But what was the magpie pecking at? Terry couldn't see anything, but the bird kept energetically pecking away, its head stabbing back and forth. Did it have some small animal trapped in the snow? He ought to go down and check it out. But it was a long way to the foot of the slope. He would lose half an hour at least.

He shook his head. He didn't have much time if he wanted to reach Hidden Lake and get back before dark. He would push on. If he found nothing at the lake, maybe he would check out the magpie on his way back.

He dug both poles into the snow and pushed forward.

# 18

"What day is it?"

Chris stared dully at the snow in front of him. He had forgotten what day it was. Mister Snowtime wouldn't tell him. He gave a harsh laugh. Mister Snowtime was all messed up.

He let his head fall back and glanced up at the air hole. Then he tried, with lifeless fingers, to twirl the branch a couple of times. Where was the sun? Someone had stolen the sun. Probably Terry. Good old Terry was always taking his things.

He let the butt end of the branch rest in its anchor hole. There was something he had to do. What was it? Oh yes, now he remembered — the hunting knife. He had to see about the knife before it was too late, before he got too weak. There was no sense in hanging on any longer. He absolutely refused to go through another night. It was altogether too much to ask.

He reached for his hunting knife and drew it out of its canvas sheath. It would take only one swift cut across his wrist, then let all the blood empty out. Or would it be better to cut his throat? He shivered. He did not see how anyone could cut his own throat. It would have to be his wrist, or better, both wrists if he could manage it.

He brought the knife up in front of his face and stared at the blade. Just a few seconds was all it took, one quick pain and all his problems would be over.

He tucked the knife under his chin and removed his gloves. For the first time he noticed how badly his fingers were swollen. They were puffed up like sausages, mottled red and blue and white. He didn't know if they were that way from the poor circulation, or from frostbite. Were they beginning to smell? Sometimes he caught a whiff of an awful stench in the hole, and wondered if his legs were rotting with gangrene. It seemed he hadn't done any running in a long time. He just didn't have the strength. And that was another thing he was afraid of — the terrible pain that must come from rotting flesh. Anyway, all that didn't make any difference now. Nothing made any difference anymore, not Mom or Dad or Terry, not anything. He had done as much as he could to survive. Didn't he have the right now to end it all?

Gently he drew the edge of the blade across his wrist. Nothing happened, and he realized that the knife edge was too dull. He would have to use considerable force to open a cut. He wasn't even sure he was strong enough. There was still another way, though. He could use the point against his heart. One swift thrust and the rest — silence, all his problems and fears over.

He tilted up the knife and teased the point through his sweater until it touched the fabric of his shirt. He gently pushed on the weapon and felt the knife tip prick his skin. A little higher — he wanted to be sure to get his heart. He tested again and felt a second cold prick of pain. That was more like it. Now he wanted one last glimpse of the outside world, a farewell look before he bowed out. If he could only see a tree, or a flower, or a bird. Oh, how beautiful the earth was and, oh, how he hated to leave! His eyes filled with tears.

He tightened his grip on the knife and waited, his gaze fixed on the air hole. He saw the mirror flash with sunlight and he braced himself for the final thrust. Then a black shadow descended on the mirror, covering it up, blocking the sun. The light darkened all around him and his head dropped to his chest. Without looking up, he knew that the red coyote had come for him. As had so often happened over these past seven days, a tired rage overtook him and he let the knife fall from his fingers. He reared back his head to yell at the coyote.

"Not yet, you're not getting me yet. I have some time left. I can hang on!"

But his gaze shrank from that red slavering mouth, that glossy dark fur, those burning eyes.

"Now, Christopher," the red coyote said. "You've been hiding from me all your life. It's time to go."

"Not yet! Not yet!" Chris screamed.

"Oh, yes, it's time. You must not keep me waiting. Come, act like a man. Act like your brother, or your father."

"Not yet . . ."

"Christopher, listen to me! There's no time left. You mustn't keep me waiting. Chris? Chris?"

"Yet . . . not . . ."

"Chris, it's too late. You must — Chris?"

Throwing back his head, Chris let out a final terrible roar of defiance, and found himself looking straight up into the face of his brother.

"*Chris!*" Terry screamed.

But Chris had passed out.

Sobbing, Terry fell to his knees and attacked the snow with his shovel.

Chris pushed away Terry's arm. "Thanks, I can manage."

Terry watched his brother stab at the road with his walking stick. Chris had spent three weeks in the hospital. He had lost two toes from his left foot and a small portion of his right heel.

"You know, Terry, you saved my life," Chris said.

"Listen, there were a hundred guys out

looking for you. I just played a lucky hunch."

"I don't mean finding me. I mean jogging." Chris's stick caught a small ridge in the road and he stumbled. "My sense of balance is all cockeyed," he complained.

"The doctors said that would happen until you got used to those missing toes. Anyway, keep walking, you're supposed to exercise your legs as much as you can."

"The doctors said if it hadn't been for my jogging exercises I would have lost both legs."

"You were smart to think of that."

"Smart? I just decided to do what I thought you would have done," Chris explained.

"Oh man, I could never have stuck it out the way you did. I would have gone crazy."

"Well, I *was* a little crazy when you found me," Chris confessed.

Terry laughed. "Boy, were you ever! You were yelling about a coyote and reciting bits of *Hamlet*. You were right off the wall, man. And, wow, did you ever stink!"

Chris grinned.

"Do you know you gave me your guns?" Terry asked.

"I really meant that," Chris said. "You can have them. I don't know if we'll ever find the twenty-two. Believe me, I'm all through hunting. There's just one thing."

"Yeah, what's that?"

"Promise me you'll never kill a magpie," Chris said.

"I wouldn't anyway. You know that crazy bird wouldn't give up. It was trying to pull the wool off the mirror. It would take a strand in its beak and pull. That made the mirror turn around and flash. That's how come I spotted the bird in the first place."

"Boy, was I lucky!"

"You better believe it. If it hadn't been for the magpie trying to gather nesting material, I would never have found the place. But you don't know how lucky you really were. Even after I saw the magpie, I wasn't about to go down there. What changed my mind was, I thought I heard a shout."

"That must have been me raving away."

Chris decided to turn around, and they headed back to the house. He drank in the view. The land rolled away below him in gentle folds. Four miles away, through a faint haze, he could see three or four flashes of white — the roofs of Salmon Springs.

He drew in a long shuddering breath. "Wow, I still can't get over how beautiful everything is."

"I'll bet," Terry said. "Hey, you ought to hear Dad going on about you. 'Greatest Feat of Endurance Ever Known in the State of Idaho,' he calls it."

Chris grinned. "Now you know how I felt when he used to brag about you."

"You're his big hero now."

"Yeah, but I have a feeling I'm not Mama's little boy anymore."

"That had to come anyway, right?" Terry said.

"I suppose. You don't hear her saying anything about my heart anymore."

"Yeah, I noticed."

Chris stopped on the road for a minute. It was still a couple of hundred yards back to the house and he was tired.

"Here," Terry said. "Put your arm on my shoulder."

"No, no, that's okay," Chris said. "I can manage on my own." Then he remembered those seven days in the snow, trying to manage on his own. "Come to think of it, I do need a little help," he said.

"Okay, kid brother, lean on me for a while."

"Happy to." Chris draped his arm across his brother's shoulder.

"Tell you one thing," Terry said. "You finally convinced me that you could walk in and out of the Snake River Canyon faster than I could."

"Oh no I couldn't," Chris argued.

"Oh yes you could," Terry insisted. "You're way tougher than I am."

"No I'm not."

They stopped then to turn and face each other. Suddenly they were both laughing, Chris holding on to Terry to keep his balance. They were still laughing when they met their mother at the door.

# If only he could have a second chance!

*Chris Palmer is always competing with his brother. Hotshot Terry, star athlete, is their father's pride and joy, and Chris is tired of being number two. But if he hadn't been trying to show up Terry, the accident would never have happened.*

*Chris was just going out for a little skiing and a little hunting. The hungry coyote seemed an easy mark, and big brother Terry had never shot one. Then the echoing crack of his rifle sets off a thundering avalanche, and Chris is buried alive under a mountain of snow. No one saw him go under. He is all alone.*

SCHOLASTIC INC.

ISBN 0-590-42267-7